The Case of the Fallen Angel

The Feline Files – Book 3

K.E. O'Connor

K.E. O'Connor Books

ISBN: 978-1-918248-10-4

THE CASE OF THE FALLEN ANGEL

Chapter 1

I was flat on my back, my tail squashed underneath me, and my paws scrabbling frantically for what felt like an eternity of dust, musty paper, and regret.

Every time I thought I was getting somewhere, another box tumbled off the shelf I'd been climbing and added its weight to my already defeated form.

I twisted my left paw, and it got jammed under something hard. Kicking out a back leg, I struck a brick. Or at least, it felt like a brick to my now numb toe beans.

I'd been so certain I was about to find the dead angel cold case based on information in the library's index card files. But it hadn't taken me long to realize it had been years since anyone had paid attention to that once excellent filing system.

But when you're as determined as I am to find your way home, you keep looking. Especially for the one case that could earn you a reprieve from being punished by the angels or, more specifically, those dozy higher angels who didn't even know what decade they lived in, let alone whether they were administering the correct punishment for crimes not committed by a charming, magically enchanted cat.

I growled as another pile of files landed far too close to my delicate ears. "Someone help!"

I'd called for assistance repeatedly until my voice cracked, but no one arrived. It was hardly a surprise. Most of the residents in the library floated around, more interested in reading ancient texts than doing anything useful. Still, I'd hoped my new fluffy companions, including Roland, who'd recently taken over the upper floor with Tabitha, might have wondered where I was and come to find me.

"Whoever's the first to help me will get a delicious treat every day for a week," I called in a voice as pitiful as I felt.

No one came. Again.

As tempting as it was to hold a pity party for one beneath this enormous, uncomfortable, foul-smelling pile of old files, I needed to take action.

I wriggled a paw, flexed my toe beans, and focused on making the boxes and files lighter. One of them shifted as a tiny spark of magic hit it. I moved my head just in time, barely a millisecond to spare, before it thumped down where my booping snooter had been.

"Focus, Juno," I muttered to myself. "You used to cast spells like this in your sleep."

Once upon a time, I'd ruled nations, with thousands of willing, and occasionally not-so-willing, subjects ready to do whatever I desired. Those days were long gone. Now, I relied on the old-school way of doing magic, and that was hard work and often led to failure.

I tried another spell. A flicker of flame shot from my paw, which I hastily extinguished. If that caught on any of these crispy old files, the building would go up in flames, and I'd be buried in the ashes.

A voice drifted through the gloom. "Good gracious! Someone's made a dreadful mess down here."

I didn't recognize the voice, but it was male and incredibly posh, which suggested it was one of the many library ghosts who flitted in and out whenever they pleased.

"Over here!" I called out. "I need help!"

"I told you there was someone down here," another voice said. That was a different ghost, but just as posh.

"Perhaps the basement is haunted," the other one said.

"Yes, by *you*!" I yelled. "Follow the sound of my voice. I'm hidden under a mountain of boxes. They're heavy, and I need help to get out from under them."

"That sounds like Juno," one of the ghosts said. "But she'd never come down here alone. Nobody goes into the basement on their own. We've all seen those frightfully realistic programs about attractive youngsters creeping down the creaking steps, never to come out again."

"Those are called movies, dear boy," the other ghost said.

"You're getting further away," I called. "Turn around and drift over here. Stay focused!"

It took several more minutes and a lot of very clear, very simple directions before I finally saw a wisp of ghostly arm shimmering in the dim light.

"You found me," I said. "Good job. Now help me get these boxes off."

"How do you expect us to do that?" one of them asked.

"Shove them. Do whatever you have to, but go carefully. I'm pinned under here, and my tail went numb hours ago."

"Ghosts don't shove stuff." There was a haughty note of disdain in the ghost's voice.

"I've seen you shove plenty of things off desks when you're in the mood." I held back the urge to snap. "And I know you throw things. You've hit me plenty of times."

"That would be Brutus. The man's an imbecile."

"You're all imbeciles," I muttered under my breath.

"What was that?"

"I said you'd be doing me a great favor by getting me out of here."

"We can't leave Juno down here on her own," the other ghost said. "How about we slide you out on a sheet of ectoplasm?"

"That sounds unpleasant," I said. "Would it even work?"

"I've never tried it, but the substance is certainly sticky enough. We could ooze some around you and then give it a good yank. What do you think?"

"I think I'll be picking ectoplasm out of my fur for days," I said. "But I'm desperate, hungry, and cold, so let's try it."

"Allow us a few moments to compose ourselves," one of the ghosts said. "We can't turn on the ectoplasmic tap whenever we desire."

That was something I was immensely grateful for, since there was already enough of the disgusting stuff lurking around the library. I was forever stepping in puddles of it.

A few minutes later, I gritted my teeth and stayed still as something cold and sticky slid around me.

"Let us know when you've got enough clinging to you," a ghost said.

I held on for another few seconds, the tacky, damp ooze forming a lake under me. "That'll do. Now pull me out."

Nothing happened.

"Are you trying?" I asked.

"This is astonishing! We can't get hold of our own ectoplasm. How curious," one of them said.

"Stay focused," I said. "Imagine it's your favorite quill in a pot of ink and you want to pick it up. I know it takes energy to lift objects, but you can do it."

There was a huff, a grunt, and a popping sound, but I remained wedged under the boxes.

"This won't do," one of the ghosts said. "The ectoplasm must have got stuck to all the paperwork rather than you."

"I promise you I'm very sticky and completely covered in ectoplasm," I said, almost losing control of my temper. "Try again."

Ten minutes passed while the ghosts circled me, discussing what to do. They lost complete track at one point and talked about horror movies for several minutes before my yelling brought them back to their senses.

"Find Roland, Minnie, or Tabitha," I said. "Bring them down here. They'll get me free."

"What a marvelous idea! Why didn't we think of that?" one of the ghosts said.

"Tabitha scares me," the other one muttered.

"Because you bother her when she's napping."

"I do enjoy a good scare. A whisk of chilly air and a quick boo, and she leaps up, hissing! It's hilarious."

"Not to her."

"Please stop talking and find my friends," I said. "If I don't get blood returning to my tail shortly, I may have to have it cut off."

"We wouldn't want that. Tallyho! Rescue is on its way, old thing."

The rescue party took thirty minutes to arrive, and by that time I was frozen and even grumpier, partly because of the cold, but mostly because I was coated in ectoplasm.

"Juno, what are you doing under there?" Minnie's adorable black-and-white face appeared, her nose twitching.

"Having a spa weekend," I said. "Sorry, I don't mean to snap, but I've been down here a long time."

"The ghosts said you'd gotten yourself in trouble," Roland added as his head popped into view. He smirked. "That's quite some trouble."

"Don't just stand there looking at me! Get these boxes off," I said.

"A please wouldn't go amiss," Roland said.

"I... Sorry. I'm embarrassed to have been defeated by paperwork. Now I know how Angel Force feels."

Roland nodded. "Come on, Minnie, let's get her upright." He set to work, efficiently kicking off boxes and shredding paperwork with his claws.

"Be careful," I said. "I was looking for another cold case file. I know it's down here somewhere. It's important to me."

"All the cold cases are important," Minnie said with a solemn note in her voice. "If you hadn't dealt with my witch's cold case, I'd still be a miserable excuse for a cat, with no friends, living off scraps and waiting to die."

"Of course they are." I finally wriggled my head free and gasped in air that didn't smell of old paper and ink. "But this is the case that'll get me home. It's a dead angel. Angel Force didn't catch the killer, so one of their own never got justice."

"What a surprise." Roland kicked another box, sending it flying. "The angels messed up."

Minnie's eyes widened. "A dead angel? You don't hear about many of those. Those big, old feathered types are almost immortal."

Roland head-butted one last box, and I was finally able to wriggle free. I flipped onto my belly and lay there for several minutes, deep breathing and letting blood return to my tail in a tingling ache of pins and needles.

"You want to solve this case?" Roland asked.

"I need to solve it," I said. "I got inside information when my angel friend Finn visited recently. He told me the angel who put me here has an unsolved death in her family history. A great-great-aunt of hers died in Badger's Haze."

Roland tilted his head from side to side, his fur gleaming. "I mean, they do sometimes die, but Minnie is right. They're really hard to kill."

"I've solved a case involving a murdered angel," I said. "But it was a shock to everyone that someone achieved such a feat."

"We can help you look for the information," Minnie said. "I was just helping Roland and Tabitha figure out the comfiest cushions upstairs, but we can put that on hold."

"What Minnie actually means is that she wants a cushion for herself and was figuring out which one to pinch when my back was turned," Roland said.

"There are plenty of cushions to go around," I said. "We have rooms full of chairs."

"Yes, but you need to find the right combination," Minnie said. "It's got to have the perfect squishiness under your paws or it won't do. They've got some great ones up on the top floor."

"Which makes it sound like you're sticking around if you need your own cushion," I said.

When I'd first discovered Minnie, she'd been a terrified, skinny shell of herself. Broken magic had damaged her, and she was full of guilt because her witch had died when she should have protected her. There'd been a time when I didn't think Minnie would make it, but it looked like we'd turned a corner.

"I like it in the library," Minnie said. "I'm definitely not looking to buy my plot in the cemetery anytime soon."

"Both of you have lived in Badger's Haze a long time," I said. "Does this case not jog your memory? After all, as Roland said, it's unusual for an angel to be killed."

They glanced at each other, then shook their heads.

"It would have been high profile," I persisted. "It must have made the newspapers and probably brought in some higher angels to investigate."

They shrugged.

"What's going on down here?" Tabitha slid into the room and headed straight for Roland.

"Juno needed rescuing. Again," Roland said.

"I barely ever need rescuing," I protested. "I got myself in a tangle with some old boxes, that's all."

"What's that all over your fur?" Tabitha asked.

"The ghosts tried to help with some ectoplasm," I said. "Tabitha, you may remember the case I'm looking for. It involved a dead angel. A great-great-aunt of someone who works for Angel Force."

"There used to be so many angels here," Minnie said. "Do you see any now? Poor old Badger's Haze has been abandoned."

"I do remember a case about an angel," Tabitha said. "She was murdered, but it was a long time ago. Maybe over a hundred years ago. It could be more."

"Anything you can remember could be useful in helping me track down the case file," I said.

Tabitha tilted her head back and gazed at the ceiling. "I remember people commenting on how sad it was. It wasn't long after her death that Badger's Haze went downhill."

"An angel getting murdered would put people off visiting," Minnie said.

"I'll tell you who will know," Tabitha said. "Morticia. If memory serves, the angel was buried in the abandoned cemetery."

I shuddered. "I'll keep looking for the file and keep Morticia as a last resort."

With my friends' help, we restored the chaos to a manageable disorder and then searched through every crate, but found nothing about a murdered angel.

Dusty, tired, and still covered in ectoplasm, I led the group back up to the main room we used in the library as our base of operations, so we could take a break and have snacks.

"There you are!" Sage sounded annoyed as she appeared on the snow globe. "I've been trying to get hold of you for ages."

I shook a strand of ectoplasm off my paw. "Are you wanting to gloat about the amazing treats Vorana has made you again?"

"No! Well, maybe. But later. This is important."

I hopped onto the desk and plucked a piece of cobweb out of my fur. "Have you finally fixed the kink in the snow globe connection, so I can see Zandra?"

"No, this has nothing to do with Zandra. I need to warn you," Sage said. "Cythera is on her way!"

Chapter 2

"Did I hear you correctly? Cythera is coming to Badger's Haze?" My whiskers brushed the snow globe as I stared at Sage in shock.

"Yes, and you need to be prepared for her visit," Sage said.

"This is incredible news!" I bounced around and twirled in a circle. "She's finally realized her mistake and gotten the higher angels to see sense. Cythera is coming here to give me my full pardon. I'm going home!" I jumped off the desk and danced around Minnie, Roland, and Tabitha.

"I can't see any fancy pants angel showing up here to do that," Roland muttered, unimpressed, as I twirled around him and playfully batted at his tail. "They're too scared to come to Badger's Haze."

"They'll come here for me." I jigged around Minnie, vibrating with excitement. "Their mistake has been uncovered. I knew this day would come. I can't wait to hear her apology."

"Isn't Cythera the angel who forced you here in the first place?" Roland asked.

"Yes! Which is why she's been sent with my pardon and a groveling apology, which I will expect to hear several times, and also put in writing so I can frame it and hang it on the wall." I bounced up and down on my paws, so excited my fur stood on end.

"Cythera isn't coming to Badger's Haze for that," Sage said, giving an irritated tut. "The higher angels are still determined to keep you there."

I stopped dancing and turned back to the snow globe. "But I've solved two cold cases Angel Force couldn't crack. And you've been giving them daily updates, encouraging them to see sense. It had to get through to them."

"I wish that were the case," Sage replied. "We've had a few higher angels in town for a conference, and I tried to get them to listen."

My flicker of joy faded. I padded back to the desk. "A conference? Are you sure? Or were they in Crimson Cove to help with the magic problems you're having?"

"As if the higher angels would help with something that mundane," Sage said. "The conference was arranged months ago. I tried to talk to them about you but they wouldn't acknowledge me."

"You are still having problems, though?" I asked.

"We're managing. That's all you need to worry about," Sage said. "Focus on the fact you've got Cythera swooping into Badger's Haze any time now."

I wrinkled my booping snooter. "Has she found out I'm looking into her relative's cold case?"

Sage shrugged. "It's possible."

"I don't know how she found out. Finn was discreet when he passed me the note about the case. Unless..." I ducked and glanced over my shoulder.

"Unless what?" Sage asked.

"Could our snow globe conversations be bugged?" I whispered. "Cythera has been listening in all this time. Maybe she even made sure the globe connected so she could monitor our conversations and make sure I wasn't breaking any rules."

"Then you've been caught, because you've been breaking plenty of rules," Sage said. "And if I recall, you've been saying some less than complimentary things about Cythera and Angel Force."

I grimaced. "Maybe she's coming to Badger's Haze to lengthen my sentence. Although the angels plan on keeping me here for the rest of my days, so that doesn't make sense."

"This angel is coming here to punish you," Minnie intoned with a deep sense of morbidness. "She's not happy with you for saying mean things about her."

I sat up straight. "I only speak the truth. And Cythera must understand my frustration about being wrongly imprisoned. That's why my tongue has been sharper than usual."

Sage chuckled darkly. "You keep telling yourself that. But it's too late now. The cat is well and truly out of the bag. If our conversations have been listened in on, she'll know everything."

"Then I've got nothing to worry about by continuing with my blunt honesty," I said. "Cythera will know I'm looking into her great-great-aunt's cold case, and that I intend to solve it and give her family resolution."

I waited a moment to see if there would be any magical explosions or furious angels dive-bombing me, but nothing happened.

"Cythera, if you're coming to Badger's Haze," I said to the ceiling, "then it must be because you want to know the truth, too."

"You know what they say about curiosity killing the cat," Sage said.

"Curiosity also uncovers mysteries and solves problems," I said. "Every warlock, witch, or magic user of note didn't get into a position of power by sitting back and letting life drift by. They tested boundaries and tried new things. They often got them wrong, but they succeeded through dogged determination. That's what I have."

"You should call it cat-ish determination," Minnie said.

"I need to find out everything I can about Cythera's great-great-aunt," I said. "Everyone else, keep looking for the cold case file."

Roland groaned. "I knew we shouldn't have come down to help."

Tabitha lightly swatted him on the head with a velvet paw. "We needed a break from redecorating. I don't mind helping Juno. She's helped us plenty."

"I'll always help," Minnie said. "Is there a treat afterward?"

"I guarantee you a tin of your favorite mixed meats if you can locate that file," I said.

Minnie bounced up and raced toward the staircase, knocking over a pile of books as she went. Roland shook his head and followed with Tabitha close behind.

"What do you intend to do?" Sage asked.

"Tabitha mentioned an angel was buried in the abandoned cemetery," I said.

Sage winced. "You want to go up against the cemetery guardian again?"

"Morticia will be busy with her sparkling new cemetery, so I'll be safe," I said.

"She'll have her magic plugged into both places," Sage warned. "You'll wind up in a coffin six feet under if you don't watch yourself."

"I'll be careful," I said. "It's almost dusk, so I can use the shadows to be discreet."

"There's nothing discreet about you," Sage said.

"I'll just look around. If I can find the angel's name, it'll help me locate her file, rather than digging through every folder and having to read the contents."

"If you make it back in one piece, tell me everything," Sage said. "I've got to go. I just heard Vorana opening a packet of ham."

"Tell Zandra I miss her," I said, "and I'll be home soon."

"If Morticia doesn't catch you." Sage's image vanished.

I headed to the main door and slipped outside. A chilly drizzle fell through the mist, dampening my whiskers and puffing up my fur. I looked like a fluffy white marshmallow as I walked through the dripping, silent streets toward the abandoned cemetery at the edge of the village.

I'd never figured out why such a small place needed two cemeteries. I'd also never asked Midnight, Morticia's fearsome familiar, why one had been abandoned in favor of the other. I could understand the need to expand, since death and taxes were the only things guaranteed, but why not expand around the original cemetery, instead of setting up a new site far away from this one?

It took me fifteen minutes to reach the cemetery. A crooked sign hung over the top of the sealed iron gate. It read: *All Hope Cemetery*. Underneath the words *All Hope*, someone had scrawled *is lost.*

Charming!

I tested the gate, but a warning ping of magic against my paw told me that forcing my way through would be unwise, so I took a slow walk around the perimeter.

The fence was intact and stood over twelve feet high, every section strongly warded to ensure no one could get inside. Or maybe it was to keep whatever was inside from escaping.

I completed my circuit and stood at the gate. I could try my new magic, but it was still temperamental, even on a good day.

"I've been watching you figure out different ways to get yourself killed ever since you got here." Midnight stepped out of the shadows, his eyes gleaming.

"Greetings!" I backed away from the gate. Depending on whether Midnight was himself or if Morticia controlled him, he could be an uncontainable force of nature. "Out for an evening stroll?"

"The second you touched the fence, I got an alert that there was trouble here." Midnight walked closer, but his tail was up, showing he meant no harm.

"I would have come to you eventually," I said, "but I didn't like to bother you, since I know how busy Morticia keeps you."

"Sure, you would." If Midnight had eyebrows, he'd have arched one. "So, what are you messing around here for?"

"It's a new cold case," I said. "I was hoping to get inside and visit a grave."

"Planning on doing necromancy with one of Morticia's corpses?" Midnight's tail twitched.

"I'm not sure I'd be able to achieve such rare magic," I said. "I've been searching for a specific cold case, but I can't find it in the library basement. I hoped I'd get a clue to the name of the deceased by visiting her grave."

"Who are you looking for? I mean, you don't know the name, but what magic did they have?" Midnight asked.

"An angel," I said. "A female angel. That's all I know. I don't know how she died or when it happened, but I know how rare angel deaths are."

"Yeah, they're tricky to kill, that's for sure," Midnight said. "What do I get if I help you?"

"My friendship isn't enough?"

Midnight smirked. "Your friendship gets me in trouble."

"You enjoy trouble," I said.

"I enjoy a quiet life, but I don't see that happening anytime soon."

"Is Morticia causing problems?" I asked.

"She may do later," Midnight said. "She's on a date. I still can't get my head around it."

"That's good! Maybe falling in love will soften her."

"She's on a date with a hexen beast. It won't end well." Midnight shook his head. "Morticia loves a bad boy, but all they do is break her heart, and she ends up cursing them."

"My wonderful witch isn't advanced in dating, either," I said.

"Is she a book geek? Or got bad teeth and lousy breath?"

"Zandra is divine, and she doesn't read, if you can believe such a horror," I said. "It's a long story, but she used a spell to grow up fast. She skipped the awkward teenage dating issues, which means she's going through them now. It's painful to watch."

"I prefer it when Morticia doesn't date," Midnight said. "When it goes wrong, she gets vicious with whoever is closest to her. Which is usually me."

"Then perhaps we should focus on something we can control." I gestured toward the closed cemetery gate.

Midnight sighed. "Why not? I've got nothing better to do than corral misbehaving skeletons. Chase rotting bones back into their coffin and stop a grumpy wraith spirit from hexing everyone." He walked to the gate, pressed both paws against it, and a huge purple flare of magic burst out, flooding the cemetery in a rippling wave of energy.

I shut my eyes against the fierce waft of power that rippled my fur.

"Hurry and get inside," Midnight said. "I need to put the wards back up. You don't want anything that's buried here creeping out."

"What kind of magic users are buried here?" I asked.

"Ones you never want to meet," Midnight muttered. "But I only know of one angel buried here, so follow me. I'll take you to her."

I dashed along the stone path, keeping a wary eye out for anything creeping about in the shadows. But the graves didn't stir.

"Here she is." Midnight stopped beside a huge, sparkling white mausoleum. An angel lay in state on the top, her wings folded against her back, hands resting on her chest.

"Cherish," I murmured, reading the inscription: *Taken too soon. Much-loved daughter, sister, and aunt to so many. She never judged. She always kept her heart open.*

The anniversary of her death was in five days. She died one hundred and fifty years ago.

I turned to Midnight. "Do you know what killed Cherish?"

"How would I know that? We get so many deaths passing through these gates."

"This one should stand out. Angels don't drop dead every day." I walked slowly around the mausoleum. There was a sparkle of magic shimmering off it to keep it looking so immaculate. "Does anyone visit Cherish?"

"Nope. Anyone who wants to come in here has to get authorization from Morticia, so we'd know if an angel wanted to pay their respects."

"If Cherish was a much-loved relative, it seems peculiar that no one would visit," I said.

"People put all kinds of waffle on those stones. What gets engraved is a reflection of the person they wish they'd been when they were alive," Midnight said.

"That has a certain logic to it," I said, "although it's a tragic one. It suggests Cherish was closed-hearted and unkind."

"Whatever goes on those stones is there forever, so you need to make yourself look good," Midnight said. "Although there are a few engravings that talk about grumpy old warlocks and surly faced witches that no one liked. I prefer those. They're honest."

"Should I risk requesting help from Morticia?" I asked. "She'll know more about everyone she looks after. And she must have gotten a boost from having an angel's power in a grave."

"Pick your moment," Midnight said. "If this date goes well, then you might survive asking her a question. But if it was a dud, you need to stay away for at least a week, or she'll curse you, stuff you in a box, and stick you in the dirt."

"I don't have a week," I said. "I'm about to get visited by Cythera from Angel Force. I hoped it was a visit to pardon me, but I fear she's learned I'm poking about in her dead relative's cold case."

"Wouldn't she be glad about that?" Midnight asked.

"Cythera isn't glad about anything I do," I said. "She's never been a fan. We formed a sort of friendship, more of a truce really, but that exploded after she sent me here."

"Huh. So, the angel who banished you to Badger's Haze is showing up. What are you going to do to her?"

"What do you mean?"

"Well, if I were in your shoes, and the angel who ruined my life visited, I'd have a little revenge party planned," Midnight said. "You could figure out a way to trap her here and make her realize what a dismal little hell pit this village is."

"I don't want revenge on Cythera," I said. "She was only following orders."

"Oh yeah, I've heard that one before. Just doing her job, was she?"

"Well, yes, I suppose so," I said. "And at first, I was raging with indignation when I arrived."

"You still are," Midnight said. "You're always complaining about being here."

"Because of how unjust it was," I said. "That's what I stand for. Righting wrongs. Fighting injustice. And this is the biggest injustice I've ever faced."

"I still favor the revenge angle," Midnight said. "Give her a taste of her own medicine. That always works."

I stared at the mausoleum. "It is odd Cythera has never been to visit. Perhaps she wasn't close to her great-great-aunt."

"Or this Cythera had something to do with her great-great-aunt's death," Midnight said. "It's easier for one angel to kill another. They know the weak spots."

I sucked in a breath. "Cythera is many things, but not a killer. Well, she was in the frame once before, but I got her off the murder charge."

"I've got you thinking," Midnight said with a chuckle. "Your spotless white angel may not be so clean-winged after all. I reckon she's coming to silence you. You're digging into her dirty laundry, and she doesn't like that."

I was about to protest when a rumble of thunder rolled overhead and a crackle of lightning slammed into the cemetery dirt.

Midnight crouched. "Uh oh. Looks like the date went badly."

"Morticia knows we're here?" I whispered.

Midnight's hackles lifted. "She knows, and she's not happy. If you value that miserable life of yours, you need to run."

Chapter 3

When I didn't move, Midnight shoved me. "I can feel Morticia taking control! If you don't go now, it'll be too late, and I won't be able to stop myself from destroying you."

With a final glance at the enormous mausoleum, I turned and ran. Mist whipped past my face as I bolted along the path, the air growing colder with each step. A low rumble rolled under my paws, and the ground trembled. A bony hand punched through the wet earth right in front of me.

I leaped over it, only for another skeletal arm to swipe at my hind legs. I hissed and twisted as more dirt-caked hands erupted around me. One hand snagged my fur. I yowled, raked it with a claw, and broke free.

I darted left, then right, paws slipping on the damp ground, until I spotted a cracked-open crypt ahead. Another skeletal hand surged up from the path and latched onto my tail. With a furious yowl, I sank my fangs into the brittle bone and shook it loose, losing my footing and somersaulting into the crypt's shadows. I slammed the heavy stone door behind me with a burst of weak magic.

I landed belly-first and lay still for a second, panting. Then I scrambled to my paws.

Deep shelves had been carved into the walls on either side of the crypt, and they'd been piled high with bones. Not complete skeletons, but it looked like someone had filed them by type. A pile of thighbones. A stack of femurs. A shelf of hands.

But what froze me solid was the wall of skulls. Dozens, maybe hundreds, lined up in neat rows. They were all looking at me. Well, I say *looking*. Skulls don't have eyes, just gaping, dark holes.

As one, they turned toward me, jaws clicking, teeth snapping.

I backed away until I hit the closed door. I glanced behind me and winced. It was no safer outside than it was in here. What was worse? Being dragged underground by grabby skeletons or hunted inside a bone vault by bodiless skulls?

"Why does Morticia hate me so much?" I muttered.

Several of the skulls' sockets lit up with an eerie glow.

"Do any of you have the answer?" I asked. "All I'm trying to do is keep Badger's Haze safe."

"Morticia didn't want to be sent here," a soft, feminine voice said from the shadows.

I jumped. "Now I have ghosts to contend with, too?"

"Not a ghost. Although... I'm not really sure what I am. Maybe I am a ghost. You could describe me as an inbetweener. How about that?"

"Are you a helpful inbetweener?" I peered into the gloom but couldn't pinpoint where the voice came from.

Two skulls tumbled from a shelf and rolled toward me, jaws chattering.

I darted sideways, dodged them, and gave one a shove with my paw.

"It's not safe for you to stay here," the voice said.

"I'm gathering that," I replied. "But I can't go back outside."

"I could help you."

I jumped over another rolling skull and gave it a kick with my back paw. "How would you do that?"

"This has been my home for a long time. I know all the routes in and out."

I yelped as a sharp pain shot down my tail. I whipped around. A skull had latched onto the very tip of my tail, its jaw clamped tight.

With a snarl, I spun, swiped at it with both front paws, my murder mittens working overtime until it finally let go and hissed at me.

"Stop biting me!" I shouted, my fur bristling. "I'm not on the menu!"

"You will be if you don't get out," the soft voice said.

"If you know an escape route, now's the time to show me," I said. "I can only play bowls with these skulls for so long."

"Why not use your magic to stop them?"

"It's a long story." I shoved another skull out of the way. This one had worryingly sharp canines. "My magic has a mind of its own."

"You do have magic though, don't you?"

"Of course. It's just... temperamental." I jumped onto the shelf with the pile of thigh bones to avoid more teeth.

"That's good. Happy news. I'll help you if you help me."

"What do you need help with?" I held a thigh bone between my front paws and played golf with the skulls, sending them spinning across the floor. But I was only slowing them. More skulls were coming for me, all glowing eyes and snapping teeth.

There was a faint shuffling from one corner, and out slid a fine-boned skeletal cat.

I drew in a breath, raising the thigh bone, ready to strike.

"No! I don't want to hurt you," the skeletal cat said.

I lowered the thigh bone as I recognized the voice. "You know the way out of here?"

She nodded. "All I need in order to show you is a tiny amount of your life force."

I narrowed my eyes. "That's all?"

"Just enough to break free from the wards keeping me inside," she said.

"Why are there wards trapping you here?" I asked. "What have you done that's so bad?"

"Nothing! It was all a misunderstanding." She gave a bony shrug. "Let's start at the beginning. I'm Tansy."

"Greetings, I'm Juno. And I'm about to be eaten alive by skulls." I whacked a persistent skull aiming for my tail. Why was it always the tail? "How much life force are we talking?"

"A drop. Just enough to give my power a boost and break through the wards," Tansy said. "It won't be difficult. The wards are old, and Morticia rarely comes here to add more magic. She's abandoned us in favor of her new cemetery. Silly cemetery guardian."

"I give you some life force, and you lead me to safety?" I asked.

"Absolutely," Tansy said brightly. "Paw promise. Like I said, I've been here a long time. I've explored every avenue. We don't have to go back into the cemetery. There's an underground route, and it leads straight to Morticia's fancy pants new cemetery."

"That doesn't sound safe to me." I clubbed away a skull that had been ambitiously hopping off the floor and snapping at my murder mittens.

"Morticia will be on her way," Tansy said. "She'll have felt the alert and will want to know what's going on."

"I don't need her catching me here," I grumbled. "Very well. But just a tiny amount."

Tansy bounced up and down, her bones clacking. "This is so exciting! It's been such a long time since I've had any energy. I survive on wisps of power that drift around this miserable place, but it's barely enough to hold my fragile bones together." She skipped over the rolling skulls and joined me on the shelf.

"I suppose you'll need some blood?" I asked. That was usually how life transference worked.

"If you'd be so kind," she murmured. "I promise I'm not greedy."

I extended my claws and squeezed them into my paw pad until a drop of blood appeared, then held it out to Tansy.

She nodded and rested her bony paw on top of mine. A white light flared between us, sending a shudder from my booping snooter to the end of my throbbing tail.

Tansy transformed. The skeleton faded, and a glorious, glossy, long dark coat covered her. She still shimmered, and she was slightly transparent, as if she were a ghost, but she was much more cat than skeleton now.

"Yummy! You have an interesting mix of magic." Tansy withdrew her paw and shook out her fur. "Old. Water and fire? And is that Crypt witch power I sense?"

"It is! You know your magic," I said.

"Well, I've been here almost as long as the planet's been spinning, so you pick up a thing or two. Come on, let's get out of here before the skulls turn us into a snack." Apparently fearless, Tansy leaped elegantly off the shelf, kicked several skulls out of her path, and barreled out of sight.

"Wait for me!" I scrambled down, jumping over snapping skulls, and hurried after her into the cobwebby darkness.

"Keep up," she called over her shoulder. "I can't wait to get out of here." Magic sparkled along the tunnel as she broke through the restraining wards with a paw flick.

"How long have you been trapped in this crypt?" I asked, avoiding holes in the dirt floor as the ground sloped away.

"You lose track of time when you do the same thing, day in and day out," Tansy said. "It might be a hundred years. It might be five hundred years. I really couldn't say."

"All this time trapped inside a crypt." I shook my head. "What did you do?"

"I got on the wrong side of the law, and the angels punished me with immortality and loneliness." Tansy blasted down another ward.

I hopped over broken stone, the ground damp beneath my paw. "You still haven't told me what you did."

"Nothing bad. You know what those angels are like. They blow things out of proportion," Tansy said.

"True enough. I've worked closely with angels over the years," I said. "I know exactly what they're like."

She slowed and looked at me, curiosity in her gaze. "Did you say your name was Juno?"

"That's right," I said.

"Oh! You're the one from the library. You really do know how terrible Angel Force is."

"Well, yes. My banishment was a big misunderstanding, too," I said. "I mean, I maybe did one or two small things wrong, but nothing bad enough to be banished to Badger's Haze."

"They're not very clever, are they?" Tansy said with a tinkle of laughter. "I kept thinking they'd come to their senses and realize what they were doing was a mistake. But when they set their minds on something, they're difficult to change. Pretty, but stubborn, and a bit air-headed."

"They can be." My opinion of Tansy grew by the second.

"Watch out for the next bit. It sometimes floods, and the mud is sticky." Tansy focused on the route.

I dodged the worst of the water, still full of curiosity as to exactly what Tansy had done to get herself trapped here, forced to be alone for eternity. That wasn't an insignificant punishment. And yes, the angels often made mistakes, as I was currently experiencing, but what if I'd just gifted life force to a dangerous criminal?

I huffed out a breath. If I had, then I could blame Angel Force. They were the reason I was stuck here, muddling through and solving the cases they weren't able to. Tansy was right. The angels were more trouble than they were worth.

"Here we are. We'll head straight up and into Morticia's home," Tansy said.

"Wait up a second," I said. "We're going into Morticia's actual home? Isn't that a suicide mission? I know you're a... well, I'm not sure what you are, but I still have some life to live."

"Morticia will be where we were," Tansy said with a joyful laugh. "She'll be looking for the cause of the disturbance in her old cemetery, while we'll be here."

"But she'll know we're here," I said. "She wards everything. She'll send Midnight after us."

"Don't worry about that grumpy old fleabag," Tansy said. "Midnight's meow is much worse than his bite."

"I wouldn't be so sure about that," I muttered.

Tansy laughed and carried on, her glossy dark tail up. She stopped beneath a small grate set into the tunnel's ceiling. Pressing both paws against it, it popped open with a fizzle of magic.

"Oh, this feels so magnificent. Follow me." She hopped up through the grate.

We entered a room with dark crimson walls, flickering candles, spooky dark corners, and the scent of moldering flowers and intense incense.

"How very Morticia," I said.

"Isn't it? She's a walking cliché of a cranky cemetery guardian. Still, she does a great job. Well, she used to at the old place. She's gotten negligent."

"It's shiny new object syndrome, isn't it?" I said. "We're all the same. The old faithful thing still works, but it's no longer fun. Then an upgrade comes along and it's bye-bye old cemetery and in with the new, exciting one."

"I suppose so."

"How do we get out of here?" I asked.

"Before we do... what were you doing in the old cemetery?" Tansy asked.

"Looking at the angel grave," I said.

"Oh! Cherish. What do you want with her?" Tansy asked.

"I want to know how she died."

"I've looked at every gravestone, mausoleum, crypt, and plot in that cemetery," Tansy said. "It's the only place I had freedom to roam. I could recite most of the inscriptions by heart."

"Were you around when Cherish died?"

"Yes. I was already in my prison," Tansy said. "I remember her being interred."

"Did a lot of people attend her funeral?" I asked.

"Barely any. Which is curious, don't you think?"

"That's very unlike the angels," I said. "They always gather in great numbers to mourn such a loss. I wonder what Cherish did to deserve to be shunned?"

"I can't tell you that," Tansy said. "But Morticia's file can."

"Morticia keeps files on all her residents?" I asked.

"Of course! There are thousands of bodies buried around here. She needs to keep track of the magic she's absorbing and work out when it'll fade into nothing."

I glanced at the closed door leading to escape and freedom. I was curious about getting Cherish's file, although I didn't want to stay any longer than necessary.

"Do you know where she keeps these files?" I asked.

"Not a clue. But why not take a look?" Tansy said. "I'm going to the kitchen to hide Midnight's food. He'll be so angry." She bounced away, laughing to herself.

A quick look around the living room told me there was nowhere to store files, so I crept into the gloomy hallway. I peeked into a few more rooms and discovered an immaculate office.

Everything was set up neatly, with not a scrap of paper on the desk. There were rows and rows of filing cabinets, and they were organized in alphabetical order.

I quickly hunted down the C section and pulled out Cherish's file. It wasn't any old file, detailing her last wishes, but her entire cold case file! Flipping it open, I found a photo clipped to the top of the first page, showing a stunning blonde angel with glinting blue eyes.

Tansy skidded into the room. "It's time to go. I caught a glimpse of Midnight prowling outside."

"I found Cherish's file!" I said.

"Perfect. So we both got exactly what we needed. I have my freedom, and you have your information on the dead angel." Tansy lifted a paw. "Shall we?"

"If Morticia has possessed Midnight, he won't let us go," I said.

"Then you'd better take hold of my paw." Tansy waggled her paw in the air.

"You think you can translocate us?" I asked.

"Let's see what your life force can do, shall we?" Tansy giggled.

There was a thump against the front door, and a spark of magic flickered under the gap. Midnight knew we were inside.

"Please don't blow us up." I connected my paw with Tansy's. "Let's go to the library."

Chapter 4

Tansy's magic rippled through me like an icy wave as the translocation spell took hold. For a heartbeat, it felt as though time had stopped. The air shimmered, magic warping and tugging around me.

Had I been foolish to trust Tansy? I'd taken her at her word that she'd bring us to the library, but I barely knew her. But what choice did I have? Stay behind and let the snapping skulls finish me off? Or face Morticia's wrath when she arrived? Neither option appealed.

My ears popped. And then we were back. The familiar scent of old books, candle smoke, and dust filled my booping snooter.

Tansy shook out her fur, glossy and semitransparent, then did a little jig on her paws before spinning in a circle.

"I didn't know I had it in me," she said. "Would you look at that? We survived! Well, you did. I'm very much not surviving these days. Some mornings, even my bones don't want to stay together."

Before I could reply, a sharp voice cut through the air.

"Who's that?" Sage's face loomed inside the snow globe.

I made the introductions, but Sage's expression didn't soften. She rarely trusted anyone new. And honestly, I couldn't blame her. My track record with new acquaintances wasn't sparkling.

"You look dull," Sage said, narrowing her eyes.

"I just survived being nearly eaten by a mob of skulls," I said. "That's enough to dull anyone's shine."

"I meant your eyes and your fur. What happened to you?"

I glanced at Tansy. "It's nothing."

"It looks very much like something to me," Sage replied. "What did you do?"

I let out a small sigh.

Tansy stepped forward. "We made a deal, but not for anything bad. I was trapped in that old cemetery and fading. It's humiliating to walk around with your bones showing. When I met Juno, I sensed her life force was unusual and thought she might help."

"Why were you stuck in the cemetery?" Sage asked sharply, already honing in on the mystery.

"It was... a misunderstanding. Let's move on, shall we?" Tansy's gaze drifted around the library. "This is so exciting! I have so much to catch up on. I bet everything's changed in Badger's Haze since I last wandered about."

"It's gone to the dogs," Sage muttered. "Maybe because of you."

"Me?" Tansy laughed, her fur rippling like mist. "All I want is a quiet retirement. And I can finally have that, in comfort, now I'm not trapped in that dreadful cemetery." She ducked as a library ghost swooped over her head, cackling.

"Tansy helped me find Cherish's cold case file," I said. "Morticia had it."

Sage glared at Tansy for a few more seconds, then shifted her attention to me. "Why would a cemetery guardian have an Angel Force case file?"

"We didn't stick around to ask her," I said. "I haven't read through the file yet, but let's not waste any time. I'll send you the case summary, and then we'll make a plan for how to solve this mysterious death."

Sage was back to eyeing Tansy, her expression cool and suspicious. "This had better be worth it."

"It will be. This is my ticket home." I pressed various buttons on the snow globe, sending a blessing to the goddess who nurtured ancient, misbehaving, enchanted globes, and sent through the information.

Case File: #32-1875
Date Filed: November 4, 1875

Victim Information

Name: Cherish
Age: 259
Address: Angel Force Assignment Housing, Badger's Haze
Occupation: Angel Force Agent:

Special Division (Possession and Demon Liaison)

Case Summary: The demon Maelor discovered the body on November 2, 1875, at the bell tower at the Church of the Spoken Grace. Cherish was pronounced dead on-site.

The scene revealed debris consistent with relic-grade halo shards scattered around. The origin of the halo is as yet unknown, but it is being looked into.

Scene Details

Location: Church of the Spoken Grace, Old Bell Tower
Weather: Cold, 41°F, light fog

Evidence Collected:

Halo shards
Singed feather samples from a wing base
Dust samples from the bell tower floor (containing spell residue)

Timeline: November 1-2, 1875
9 a.m.–3:30 p.m.: Cherish working with her new informant, Maelor
3:30 p.m.: Nix Busby seen visiting Cherish

4 p.m.–9:30 p.m.: Working with Maelor
9:30 p.m.: Assumed on break (not confirmed by anyone)
11:55 p.m.: Cherish seen entering the bell tower
12:10 a.m.: Shouting heard from the bell tower
12:15 a.m.: Body discovered by Maelor
1 a.m.: Angel Force arrives on the scene

Persons of Interest/Witnesses

Maelor (demon): Cherish's informant on demonic relic trafficking.
Lumiel (angel): Celestial custodian of relics. Worked with Cherish on recent artefact finds.
Nix Busby (witch): Local socialite and the head of the Badger's Haze Social Society. Seen with Cherish the day she died after a disagreement over a necklace.
Aurek (angel): Angel Force Oversight Officer assigned to Maelor to ensure compliance.
Yahir Hallow (warlock): Historical consultant.
Verity (angel): Trainee at Angel Force academy, shadowing Cherish. Also, Cherish's cousin.

Chapter 5

"It's rare you find any angels who'll negotiate with demons," Sage said, after we'd all read through the case summary.

"It used to be more popular," I agreed. "When the angels believed they could find goodness in anyone."

"I can't remember the last time I met an angel negotiator who worked with demons," Sage said. "They used to have a task force that specialized in this work, but there were too many deaths, so they put the program on hold."

"That's because demons are beyond saving," Tansy said with a definitive nod. "Some people are just made to be bad."

"Does that include you?" Sage asked.

A movement near the ceiling caught my eye. A large white feather floated down through the library air and landed gently on the desk beside me.

"If I ever needed a sign to investigate this cold case, I've just received it," I said.

"Or it could be the library ghosts playing with you," Sage said.

I sniffed the feather. It smelled of old magic and spun sugar.

"Cherish needs her murder solved," I said. "We must figure out which of the suspects ended her life."

A tremulous pounding echoed through the library. It came through the main door. Loud, steady, and insistent.

"Morticia has found you," Sage said.

"She wouldn't leave the cemetery just to give me a mild reprimand." I hurried to the window and peeked through a curtain gap. There was no Morticia, but the thudding didn't stop.

"You'd better go down and calm her," Sage said. "Or she'll set the corpses on you and then burn down this library."

I grimaced, but moved. I hadn't even made it to the top of the stairs when the sound of splintering wood rang out, then footsteps marched steadily toward me, heavy and sure.

I lifted my booping snooter and sniffed the air. It wasn't the grounded, earthy scent of a cemetery guardian. It was sugar and cinnamon.

The feet pounded up the stairs, growing closer. I backed into the room.

"Find a place to hide!" Sage advised.

"It's not Morticia," I whispered. "It's Cythera."

"So much for you getting a sign to investigate the case," Sage said with a sigh. "You're about to get a rap across the toe beans."

"Juno, don't you hide from me! I know you're staying here." Cythera marched into the room.

I was crouched behind a book stack with Tansy, but decided to brave it out. I stood tall and stepped forward to meet Cythera.

"Greetings! I'm glad you finally remembered to visit your prisoner."

Cythera was her usual uptight, radiant vision of angelic perfection, with flawless skin, dazzling blue eyes, and golden hair that shimmered under the library's flickering lights. Her wings were extended, a clear sign she was unhappy to see me.

Before she'd marched in, I'd concealed Cherish's case file inside a copy of *The World Encyclopedia of Witch Wars*, just in case that was the reason for her visit.

"How have you been?" I asked when she didn't speak.

"Stressed. No thanks to you." Cythera looked around the library with thinly veiled disgust.

"How can I possibly cause you stress when I'm tucked away here, harming no one?"

"You always cause harm," Cythera said.

"Let me introduce you to a few people." I gestured to Tansy. "This is my new friend, and there are other familiars living here, too. We've formed a nice little community."

Tansy remained hidden, her eyes shut as she tried to make herself look small.

"I'm not here to discuss your weird friendships," Cythera snapped.

"Then why are you here?" My gaze flicked to the encyclopedia.

Cythera pressed her lips together. "It's time for your assessment."

I drew in a sharp breath. "You're here to see if I'm ready to be released? That's perfect news! I was just saying—" I stopped myself before revealing too much. No need to let Cythera know I'd been communicating with Sage. "I mean, I've been chatting with the library ghosts about how much everyone must be missing me in Crimson Cove."

"You're barely mentioned," Cythera said. "And the place is a lot quieter without you."

"Not from what I've heard."

Her gaze narrowed. "How do you know what's going on in Crimson Cove? Part of your punishment is to be cut off from all forms of external communication. I even told Finn not to speak to you when he picked up that criminal."

"Finn behaved impeccably," I said. "And it's thanks to me you have that criminal. I'm doing excellent work to prove my value. Not that I should have to. I'm an essential part of Crimson Cove's freelance law enforcement crack team."

"You're an unnecessary pain in my behind." Cythera folded back her wings with a rustle of feathers. "I'm still getting weekly visits from the higher angels because of your recklessness."

"Once you've done your assessment and seen I'm the perfect model cat-izen," I said brightly, "you'll allay their fears and I can come home. I'll start helping again."

Cythera grunted.

"You are happy I've been solving these cold cases, aren't you?" I asked.

"It's always good to have a resolution. What are you working on now?" Her tone was light, but Cythera had never been good at lying.

"I'm undecided," I replied. "There are so many cases left to fester in the library basement. Is there any case in particular you'd like me to work on next?"

"Show me the basement," Cythera said.

"Why do you want to see down there?"

"Because you're meddling with confidential information that has nothing to do with you," she said. "I want to make sure you're being respectful."

"I'm always respectful when dealing with crime."

Cythera pressed her lips together again. "I'll find the place myself if I have to."

"No! No! I'm happy to show you. But I'm still curious," I said. "If you're here to assess me, why do you want to look at the files?"

"Because you've tangled yourself up in our business again," Cythera said. "No one asked you to look into the cold cases."

"I had to do something useful while stuck here," I said. "And you know your key performance indicators will trend up thanks to me solving these crimes."

"The basement?" Cythera turned and looked toward the stairs.

I continued, "Not only did I trap an ancient, powerful, monstrous magical creature in an enchanted well, one that has troubled Badger's Haze for many hundreds of years, but I also helped capture a cold, callous, and ruthlessly brilliant criminal. You may even get a commendation for all of my hard work."

"Show me the cold cases," Cythera said through gritted teeth.

I hurried toward the stairs with Cythera stomping behind me like thunder. "I've been so busy, I haven't had time to tidy. And there was a minor incident earlier today."

"What kind of incident?" Cythera asked as she followed me into the building's depths.

"I was searching for a file, and one or two boxes fell on me. Don't worry. My ego was the only thing that suffered damage." I peeked around the corner into the basement and failed not to gasp.

Although we'd made a start on tidying, it hadn't been a thrilling task, and we'd left the library ghosts to it. After all, how much damage could they do?

Lots.

Files lay scattered in precarious piles, pages fluttered, and ectoplasm tangled everywhere like the aftermath of a magical ferret rave.

"Show me." Cythera pushed past and took in the scene. She inhaled deeply through her nose, then let out a long, slow exhale through her mouth.

"It's not as bad as it looks," I offered. "I have my own filing system."

"You're messing everything up. Why do you always do this?" Cythera's voice was tight with frustration. "Never mind. Which case are you looking into?"

"Why do you care?" I asked.

"Because you could be stirring up trouble, and that's the last thing we need," Cythera replied. "I've got enough going on in Crimson Cove without being sent here to check on you."

"If things are so hectic in Crimson Cove, you could have postponed your visit," I said. "I assume you keep tabs on me, anyway."

"I'm too busy to spy on you."

I tilted my head as I studied her. Why wasn't Cythera asking about her great-great-aunt's cold case? If she wanted a progress report, I'd gladly tell her I'd found the file. What was really going on?

"You could have suggested the higher angels visit," I said. "Or is that beneath them? Perhaps they're too embarrassed to face their mistake."

"At this rate," Cythera muttered, "I'll have a higher angel moving into my home to make sure I'm not completely incompetent."

"Your charming husband wouldn't like that," I said. "How is the adorable Maverick?"

She looked away. "We're on a break."

"That's terrible news. He's a sweetheart."

"Yes, well, we're not always what we seem, are we?"

"I'm sure you can fix any problem," I said. "Was it your decision or his?"

"That's none of your business. I'm busy with work. And Maverick's not as charming as everyone thinks. Get this mess cleared up," Cythera said, switching topics. "Make sure everything is properly filed and on a shelf by the time I return in the morning."

"That's a lot of work," I said. "You're welcome to stay and assist. We can get food and catch up. How's Zandra? I miss her."

"I need to sleep."

"You can stay here. There's plenty of room," I offered. "Although it's damp, and the roof leaks when it rains."

"I'm not staying here with you and your new bunch of misfits. I booked a room at the local inn. I'll be back at dawn to check in on your progress." She turned and stomped toward the stairs.

I scrambled after her. "Are you sure there's nothing I can do to help with Maverick? It's always good to talk these things through."

"Not with you, it isn't." Cythera marched through the gaping hole she'd made in the library's front door.

I stared after her, my heart pounding. Cythera had lied. This visit wasn't about an assessment to determine if I was rehabilitating into a model familiar. She knew I'd reopened her great-great-aunt's cold case.

Maybe Morticia had told Cythera someone was snooping around. But would that grumpy old cemetery guardian help Cythera? I had to know for sure.

Leaping over the pile of broken wood, I slipped outside. Cythera's tall, glowing form loomed in the distance as she strode along the street.

I dashed after her, careful to stay low and out of sight.

Cythera kept marching, her pace brisk, and every so often her wings flared wide as if she fought her inner fury. Instead of stopping at the only inn in Badger's Haze, a small, run-down place with a layer of grime on the windows, she walked past it and kept going.

As she continued, I realized she was headed to the abandoned cemetery.

Cythera halted outside the gate and stood there for several minutes, staring into the darkness beyond the rusted bars.

I crouched low and watched her. Cythera was here because her ancestor's death was being examined. Was there something about the death that Cythera didn't want anyone to find?

I turned and raced back to the library, my paws skimming over the path, heart hammering with urgency. By the time I reached the desk, I was breathless and panting.

Tansy was settled beside the snow globe, peering in at Sage.

"I thought Cythera might have vaporized you," Sage said. "What happened in the basement?"

"Cythera told me to clean it up," I said. "But that's not important. She's gone, but I followed her. She went to the cemetery where her great-great-aunt was buried."

Tansy yawned and blinked sleepily. "Maybe she wants to pay her respects. Can we do this in the morning? All this excitement has worn me out."

"There's no time for sleep. Sage, I'm sending you the first suspect in Cherish's murder." I pressed my paw to the globe's base and took a steadying breath. "We need to find out what secrets Cythera doesn't want uncovered before she stops us for good."

ANGEL FORCE INTERVIEW TRANSCRIPT

Case file: #32-1875
Conducted by: Angel Gideon
Interviewee: Maelor

GIDEON: Please state your full name and origin for the written record.
MAELOR: I am Maelor. I was born in the infernal province of Netherfold, a region far removed from these gentler lands, and a place I don't care to return to.
GIDEON: You were granted provisional sanctuary under Angel Force law in exchange for sensitive intelligence concerning demonic relics and trafficking routes. Is that correct?
MAELOR: It is. The terms were made clear when I arrived. I provide information, names, and locations, all connected to the movement of forbidden relics. In return, I'm permitted to dwell here without threat of immediate annihilation. While not precisely what I would call hospitality, it has been manageable.
GIDEON: Describe your relationship with Cherish.
MAELOR: We had a professional understanding. She possessed a rare quality among angels. An interest

in truth, even when that truth was unpleasant. She did not see me as a beast to be feared nor as an enemy to be extinguished, but as a source of knowledge, one which she used wisely. She sought answers concerning relics tainted by infernal magic, and I provided what I knew.

GIDEON: When did you last see Cherish?

MAELOR: On the night of her death. We had arranged to meet near the bell tower of the old church. There was a relic she wished to speak about. I arrived late, and before I could enter the tower, I saw her silhouette near the top, and I heard raised voices. Someone was with her. I couldn't make out the words, but the tone was angry.

GIDEON: Did you see who she was speaking to?

MAELOR: No. I saw only shadows. One of them moved suddenly. And then Cherish fell. She struck the ground with such force I knew immediately she couldn't have survived. I ran to her side, though I knew it was useless.

GIDEON: You didn't enter the bell tower to see who had attacked Cherish?

MAELOR: I didn't. I was shocked by what had happened.

GIDEON: Did you see anyone leave?

MAELOR: I kept my head down. I'm

not proud of this, but I feared that being discovered would do me no favors, especially given my situation.

GIDEON: You didn't want to get injured by whoever threw Cherish out of the tower?

MAELOR: I'm not powerful. Someone slayed Cherish, so I would be a bug to them. They'd have squashed me without hesitating.

GIDEON: Do you have knowledge of the relic fragments found at the scene?

MAELOR: It's part of a celestial halo tied to the old order of divine enforcers. Cherish feared it had fallen into the wrong hands, perhaps been corrupted. I confirmed that there were rumors of demons coming into possession of these fragments. They were actively looking for more.

GIDEON: For what purpose?

MAELOR: They planned to misuse them. Cherish must have had the piece of halo on her when she died. It shattered when she hit the ground.

GIDEON: What would motivate someone to kill Cherish?

MAELOR: Cherish knew things, too much, perhaps. She walked a line between light and shadow. Some of your kind believe such angels lose their purity. Others simply find them inconvenient or an embarrassment.

GIDEON: You're suggesting an angel did this?

MAELOR: There are few powerful enough to kill an angel. I know I don't have the magic to do so.

GIDEON: Do any names come to mind?

MAELOR: It's not for me to interfere in the affairs of angels.

GIDEON: But you believe it was an angel arguing with Cherish?

MAELOR: I didn't see, but perhaps. I'm not making guesses. I understand her work troubled some. That is all I can say without straying into make believe.

GIDEON: You're to remain in Badger's Haze until this matter is concluded. Any deviation will be considered a breach of your sanctuary terms, and our protection will be lost. Do you understand?

MAELOR: Understood. I am sorry this has happened. I may be a demon, but I mourn her loss. Cherish was one of the rare few who treated me as more than a monster.

FOLLOW UP: Verify Maelor's presence at the bell tower: Maelor claims to have been outside the bell tower at the time of Cherish's death, but no witnesses currently corroborate this. Given his origin and dubious background, this remains a weak alibi.

Although cooperative, Maelor's account is notably careful. His admission of loyalty to Cherish may be genuine, but his omission of details suggests he is concealing something.

Flag Maelor for secondary questioning following the completion of the first round of interviews.

Assessment of relic fragments: Cherish was investigating a fragment of an angelic halo. This is an extreme rarity, and its shattered state is of concern. Maelor confirmed its divine origin, but details remain vague.

Send the relic shards for analysis at the Sanctum Archivum. Confirm its origin and potential for misuse.

Review Cherish's recent work: Maelor reports Cherish feared betrayal from within Angel Force. We must investigate this with discretion. Pull all internal communications, mission logs, and correspondence Cherish submitted in the last twelve months.

Chapter 6

"A dubious demon with no alibi, and Maelor was there when Cherish died." I sat beside the snow globe with the case file open.

Sage snorted. "Angel Force should have charged him. Surely, he's the most obvious suspect."

"I need to speak with him, but I've heard of no demons living in Badger's Haze," I said. "He must have left the village."

"There are a few demon bones in the cemetery," Tansy said.

"But no actual demons living freely around here?" I asked.

Tansy shrugged. "Why would they? The pickings are slim."

"Don't you have a problem to solve before you figure out how to interview Maelor?" Sage asked.

I glanced up from squinting at the aged paper. "What would that be?"

"The giant, unfriendly angel stomping around who won't let you loose on this investigation."

"I've got a plan for that," I said. "First things first. We need to find out where Maelor lives. I'll need your help with that."

"What trouble are you getting me into this time?" Sage asked.

"No trouble. But find a way to connect me to the Crypt witches in Willow Tree Falls. They know everything about misbehaving demons. It's possible Maelor ended up in the prison beneath their cemetery. They keep track of all the demons who come their way."

"Give me ten minutes," Sage said, and she vanished from sight.

I turned to Tansy. "Do you remember anything about Maelor when he moved here to work with Cherish?"

"I do! He wasn't popular, but he never caused trouble," Tansy said. "Maelor was respectful. I got the impression he wanted to help."

"What made him turn on the other demons?" I asked.

Tansy wrinkled her nose. "I wasn't that friendly with him. We all kept a safe distance. Demons can be vengeful, so maybe someone did him wrong, and he decided to get what he could out of Angel Force."

"I've met more than a few demons," I said. "They want something out of every deal they make. They never do anything out of the goodness of their hearts."

"The angels were protecting him," Tansy said. "They gave him a place to live and set repellent wards around the village, so if any other demon tried to get in, they'd be alerted. It was a kind of safe house, I guess."

"Maelor must have had valuable information for the angels to look after him so well," I said.

"There were high-profile arrests after he defected," Tansy said. "It made the residents a little warmer to him, knowing the streets were safer because of those captures."

Sage's face reappeared in the snow globe. "We've only got a few minutes. I don't know how long I can keep this connection open, so no waffle. I've already told Tempest what you're up to."

I focused on the globe. The image was so fuzzy that if Sage hadn't told me I was looking at Zandra's older sister, Tempest Crypt, I'd have been none the wiser. "Greetings! It's been a while."

"Yeah, no kidding," Tempest said in her usual blunt manner.

"Can you help with our demon problem? What details do you need?"

"Sage has given me the basics. Maelor served part of his sentence here, but he's been out on probation for a long time."

"What did he do to end up in your prison?" I asked.

"He blew up a bank. He also tried to suck out half a dozen souls."

"Maelor reverted to his former demon ways," I muttered. "Do you have a location for him?"

"Of course. We track the troublemakers who pass through here," Tempest said. "But from what I understand of your own sentence, you can't get out of Badger's Haze to interview him."

"Can you send him to me?" I asked. "You could make it part of his probation agreement."

"Yeah, I can arrange something," Tempest said. "Give me tonight to work on it. I should have it sorted by the morning."

"I appreciate that," I said. "This is the case that could get me out of here and back to Zandra, so I'm determined to crack it."

"Make sure you do. She hasn't been the same since those numb-skull angels separated you. She came by here a while back, and it was like some demon had sucked her energy away. She was so angry. Blaming Angel Force. Me! Everyone. Let me know if..."

The connection fuzzed away, and Sage's face returned.

"Did you get everything you needed?" Sage asked.

"Almost. There's one more thing. You were right about Cythera being a roadblock in this investigation. We need to distract her."

"What have you got in mind?" Sage asked.

"Issue an invitation to the wonderful Maverick. Suggest he drops into Badger's Haze so they can have some alone time to talk over their problems."

"That's a lousy thing to do," Sage said. "That poor guy doesn't deserve the sharp edge of Cythera's tongue for showing up uninvited because you roped him into one of your schemes."

"It's not a scheme! It's a well-thought-out genius plan that will guarantee a killer is caught." I shrugged at her skeptical expression. "Besides, maybe they'll reconcile while he's here. Tell him to make a romantic gesture."

"Cythera loathes romance. Or have you forgotten how much she grumbled and grouched when getting married?"

"Their relationship needs shaking up. Cythera needs to realize what she's missing out on," I said. "And I have to solve this case. You've seen how tied my paws are with Cythera breathing down my neck. I need to do something I'm less than proud of for the greater good."

"You'll owe Maverick an apology after this."

"And I'll make a most sincere one," I promised.

"I'll see what I can do. But I won't be able to get him there until tomorrow."

"That gives me time to review the case notes, and Tempest time to order Maelor here so I can question him."

"Get some sleep. I'll be in touch." Sage signed off.

Tansy, who'd been watching the whole thing, stretched out. "Is this what you do every day?"

"Most days I snack and nap," I said. "It's not always this exciting."

"It seems terribly exciting to me," Tansy said. "You're solving murder cases. Helping so many people."

I tilted my head from side to side. "Honestly, I'm mainly helping myself. I've been separated from my bonded witch, and I'll do anything to get back to her. Break rules, smash through realms, mess with Angel Force. After all, they messed with me."

"Oh, I know all about that," Tansy said. "And I was glad that angel you brought here didn't recognize me. My face was on wanted posters for years."

"Remind me again what you did to get on the wrong side of the angels?" I asked.

"I forget. Why don't we get some sleep?" Tansy hopped off the desk and floated away.

⚜ ❧

I was up bright and early, having breakfasted out of an old tin of sardines.

Tansy watched me eat but didn't join in.

"I miss food," she murmured. "It's one of the few downsides of being this way. But I'll never forget that yummy mouthfeel of a tasty morsel of meat. It looks like you enjoyed that meal."

"The tin's contents were two years out of date, but it filled a hole." I tapped the snow globe. "What's keeping Sage? We need to get this case solved."

I had a quick whisker wash and then wandered to the top floor, looked in on how Roland and Tabitha's renovation works were going, then skulked down to the cold case storage area. I spent five minutes tidying, then headed back to the snow globe, happy to see Sage's face when it came into focus.

"Is Maverick on his way?" I asked.

"The poor guy is buying an extra-large cactus as we speak as a gift," Sage said with a shake of her head. "He was so excited when I lied and told him Cythera missed him and wanted to talk. I felt bad."

I winced. "Maverick is awfully innocent. It's one of the many things I like about him. His perfect naivety."

"If this goes wrong, you'll owe both of them a serious apology."

"I'll make it up to them," I said. "They're a good couple. I don't want to see them apart."

"Cythera's stressed from all the extra work," Sage said. "Maverick's barely gotten a look-in for weeks."

"Because of the magic problems?" I asked.

"Among other things. Anyway, he's on his way. He'll be in Badger's Haze within the hour." Sage glanced away. "Tempest is attempting to come through. She must have news for you."

"The morning just keeps getting better," I said.

I had to wait a few more minutes before a fuzzy image of Tempest appeared in the globe.

"I got you what you need," she said without wasting a second on pleasantries. "Maelor is heading to Badger's Haze now. He wasn't happy, but I told him he had no option unless he wanted back inside."

"Thank you. Maelor was Angel Force's prime suspect, so it makes sense to start with him."

"I rarely say this about demons," Tempest said, "but go easy on him. He's had a rough go of things. The state he was in when I found him surprised me. He's not doing well on his own."

That comment shocked me. Tempest never showed sympathy toward demons. Most of them spent their time trying to ruin her life, destroy her family, or escape prison. So, for her to feel sorry for Maelor... well, he must be in a bad way.

I said my goodbyes and left the library with Tansy. As usual, the sky was gray, and a chilly drizzle dampened the air, keeping residents indoors.

"I'll stay away from the demon suspect, if that's okay with you," Tansy said. "I thought I'd explore Badger's Haze. See what's new."

"Most of it is decaying," I said. "There's little to see, so don't be too disappointed."

"It's been such a long time since I've been above ground, everything will feel like a novelty. I'll see you later, back at the library." She bounced away on her ghostly paws, leaving me to make the rest of the journey to the edge of the village.

Before I even reached the boundary, I felt a warning buzz from the wards, reminding me not to take too many more paw-steps unless I wanted to be zapped into next week.

"I hear you," I muttered. "I'm not trying to get out. But I want someone to get in, so play nice."

The boundary wards hummed again, almost like a growl, making my fur fluff with the static.

After a few minutes of waiting, the air on the other side of the boundary shimmered, and a small, hunched-over demon with gray, scaled skin, wearing a ragged dark coat, stumbled through. He yanked the coat tighter around himself and grimaced as he looked around, his gaze eventually settling on me.

"Greetings. I'm Juno," I said.

He nodded. "Maelor. Tempest sent me here. On pain of death."

"She has a wonderful way with words," I said. "Thank you for being so cooperative."

Maelor grunted. "Didn't you miss the pain of death part?"

"I thought we'd take a walk to the old bell tower."

He hunched over even more. "Do we have to? I can talk to you here."

"It could jog your memory," I said. "You know why I wish to speak with you, don't you?"

"Tempest said it was about Cherish's death, right?"

"Yes. I've reopened her case, and I'm investigating to find out what happened to her."

Maelor sighed, and a small plume of smoke drifted from his wide nostrils. "That was a long time ago. My memory's not what it used to be."

"Which is why visiting the scene of the crime might help you get clarity," I said.

Maelor let out another breath and gave a reluctant nod. "Cherish was decent to me, so I suppose I owe her." He pressed a clawed hand against the ward and stepped through without trouble.

I glared at the boundary line. If only it were that simple for me.

Maelor shook out his hand and flexed his fingers a few times. "There's no demon objection ward anymore. There used to be. Back when I lived here."

"I imagine Angel Force set that up to protect you from intruders." I fell into step beside him as he shuffled forward, his movements stiff and slow.

"That feels like another lifetime ago," Maelor said. "Back when I was helping others."

"Why did you help the angels instead of your own kind?"

"It's a story as old as time," Maelor said. "I was mistreated, and I wanted revenge. The angels made me a deal. A chance at a new life. Everything paid for. A home of my own."

"That sounds tempting," I said.

"It was all thanks to Cherish. She was so persuasive. Not pushy or mean, but she talked sense." He stopped outside the small wooden gate that led to the bell tower. His gaze lifted. "This place hasn't changed."

"It's one of the few structures I haven't explored," I said.

Maelor looked down at me, his eyes dull. "Why are you here? When I asked, Tempest said it was none of my business and to answer all your questions."

"I'm righting wrongs. Shall we?" I gestured to the gate.

He grunted, then pushed it open with his hip and trudged inside.

"I read your interview with Angel Force," I said. "Where were you standing when you saw Cherish fall?"

"Over to the right. I can show you if you like." Maelor continued forward slowly and stopped. "Right about here."

I moved beside him and looked up at the bell tower. From this angle, he'd have had a perfect view through a carved opening. "What did you see when you looked up?"

"I saw Cherish. She was arguing with someone, just like I told Angel Force."

"You didn't glimpse that person?"

Maelor shook his head. "I only saw her. But I could tell she was angry. Her wings were flared, and she was gesturing."

"You didn't think to help?"

He shrugged. "She was a powerful angel. Not afraid to face down trouble. She didn't need me."

"Then what happened?" I asked.

"If you've read my statement, you already know. She fell. Or was pushed. I didn't see. But suddenly, she was falling. I ran to save her, but I was too late."

"Did she try to fly?" I asked.

"Her wings seemed stuck," Maelor said. "Like she couldn't get them open. She was moving her arms and legs, but her wings were locked into place."

"It's a high point to fall from," I said. "But Cherish was an angel. She should have survived that fall."

"None of it made sense." Maelor looked away. "I kept wondering if I could have done anything else, but she was gone. Just like that. One minute she was in the bell tower, then she was falling, and then she was dead."

"Did you go into the bell tower to stop her killer?"

"I stayed with Cherish. I wanted to help her. Or at least let her know she wasn't alone."

"And you didn't see anyone running away? Hear anything?"

Maelor hunched into himself. The silence stretched. Witnessing a death would shake anyone, but this was a demon, and they didn't shock easily.

"I'm not the most powerful demon," he finally said. "I wasn't then, and I'm definitely not now. Back then, I was more like a sidekick. Someone they sent to fetch things. Do the grunt work."

"And you didn't like that?"

"The angels gave me a chance at something else. A life with dignity. Cherish saw potential in me when no one else did." Maelor's gaze moved to the tower's peak. "She could be quirky. Odd. Different from every other angel I'd met. But she saw me. Really saw me. So yeah, I owed her a lot."

"I'm glad she was there for you," I said.

"Not that it mattered. Once she was gone, I lost my way," Maelor muttered. "That's how I ended up in the Crypt Witch prison. And I'll probably end up back there. I'll die in a cell. No one will miss me."

"I'm sure that's not true."

"It is! And I'm fine with it." Maelor shoved his hands into his coat pockets. "I know Angel Force thinks I did this, but there was never any evidence. I promise you I had nothing to do with what happened to Cherish."

The sincere note in his voice surprised me. "Are you able to stay in Badger's Haze for a few days? I might have more questions."

"Tempest said I can stay the week. Then I have to get back to my probation duties," Maelor said. "Although she also said this visit counts toward my probation hours served, so that's something."

"That was surprisingly generous of her," I said. "Where are you staying?"

"There's an inn nearby. I think I remember it from the last time I was here."

I fought back a smile. He'd be checking into the same place Cythera was staying. If their paths crossed, that could be interesting. Maybe they'd have breakfast together and swap stories. Or fight each other to the death. It could go either way.

"I'll be in touch if anything comes up," I said.

Maelor nodded and shuffled off, his coat flapping in the wind as he disappeared into the misty gray morning.

I stayed where I was, my thoughts swirling. A lowly demon, protected by Angel Force, abandoned by his own kind, grieving a fallen friend. Demons had an intrinsically tricky nature. Some tried to be good, and sometimes they managed for a while. But mischief ran in their blood. It was part of who they were.

Was Maelor telling the truth? He'd been here. He'd seen Cherish fall. Could he have been the one who pushed her?

Maybe I just needed the right incentive to get him to admit what had happened all those years ago. Then, we could finally solve this case. And I could go home.

Chapter 7

"Maelor doesn't sound like much of a demon." Sage lounged close to an empty plate of smoked salmon she'd rather cruelly eaten in front of me as we'd discussed my meeting with Maelor.

"He was a pathetic figure," I said. "I suppose spending time in the Crypt Witch prison never does you any favors. He appeared broken. And he wanted to go nowhere near the bell tower. He seemed sad about what had happened to Cherish."

"He was laughing on the inside," Sage said. "Demons are always trouble. It's got to be him."

I nodded, my gaze on the case file. "Maelor was there when Cherish fell. What if he'd been the one arguing with her and damaged her wings before shoving her out of the tower? What did they argue about?"

"He most likely did it to amuse himself," Sage said.

Tansy glided over on her ghostly paws and joined us. "I'm happy to see the demon didn't eat you."

"Maelor didn't even try," I said. "He told me he lost his way after Cherish was murdered and started messing up. That was how he ended up in prison."

"You can't trust a demon," Sage said. "Keep working on him and get a confession."

"I will. He's sticking around Badger's Haze for now," I said. "While I figure out a way to crack him, let's look at the other suspects interviewed."

Before I could send through any information to Sage, the door banged open, and Cythera marched up the stairs and into the room.

Tansy squeaked and vanished from sight.

Cythera's fierce, icy gaze latched onto me, sending a shiver to my tail tip. "Why did you bring him here?"

"Greetings. Who are we talking about?" I asked as innocently as possible.

"You know who!" Cythera jabbed a finger at me. "I've been telling that irritating husband of mine to go away for the last half hour, but he insists I want him here."

"It's important that you have open communication channels with Maverick," I said. "How else will you resolve this minor tiff?"

"It's not a minor tiff. And it's also none of your business." Cythera's gaze cut to the snow globe. "Why are you always lurking around that thing?"

I glanced back, glad to see Sage was nowhere to be seen. "It keeps me warm."

Cythera's forehead wrinkled. "Tell Maverick to leave. He won't listen to me. And he's brought a cactus with him that's so big he nearly poked his eye out on the thorns."

"That's a love gift," I said. "It matches your character."

"Stop messing around in my affairs." Cythera's wings snapped out. "You're in enough trouble as it is."

"By solving two cases Angel Force couldn't crack?" I flicked my tail. "Why would that get me in trouble? Most divisions would have given me a medal and a key to the town."

"The only thing you're getting is time behind bars if you don't stop meddling," Cythera said.

"Stop worrying about me and make sure everything is fine with your charming husband," I said.

"Everything will be fine. I'll sort that out when I have enough time," Cythera said.

I narrowed my eyes. She was vexatious today. "What about the rest of your family? Perhaps they could assist you to return to wedded bliss. Are you close to any relatives in particular? Any great-great-aunts, maybe?"

Cythera's nostrils flared. "I'm going to check the cold case storage, so it had better be tidy."

"It's a picture of perfection," I called as she retreated, before turning back to the snow globe. "It's safe. You can come out."

"I told you sending Maverick to Badger's Haze was a terrible idea." Sage poked her nose into view. "That's another black mark against your name. How will you ever get out of that place if you keep irritating Cythera?"

"I'm irritating to her no matter what I do," I said. "Now, let's look at the next suspect. I'm sending you Nix Busby's interview."

ANGEL FORCE INTERVIEW TRANSCRIPT

Case file: #32-1875
Conducted by: Angel Gideon
Interviewee: Nix Busby

GIDEON: Please state your full name and magical designation for the official record.
BUSBY: I'm an enchantress. I specialize in event magic, charm work, and atmosphere spells. If there has been a gathering of any significance within the celestial or mortal realms in the last fifty years, the chances are I was responsible for its success.
GIDEON: And your place of residence?
BUSBY: I've had a few residences over the years, but I live in the manor house on Port Obsidian Close. Badger's Haze is my home.
GIDEON: You were acquainted with Cherish, is that correct?
BUSBY: We were friends. Not tell-your-secrets, paint-each-other's-nails friends, but I was fond of her. And she had wonderfully entertaining stories she'd tell at my parties. She was a fabulous guest. Quirky, but always kind to me.
GIDEON: When did you last see her?
BUSBY: The day she died, actually. I

returned a necklace she'd lent me for a soirée. It was a gorgeous silver piece, terribly divine. It matched my gown perfectly, and she was always happy to share.

GIDEON: There was mention of an argument because you didn't want to return the necklace.

BUSBY: Such a scandal and entirely untrue. I perhaps kept the gorgeous creation for longer than promised, but not because I wanted it forever. Well, I did. I had so many parties to attend, and it went perfectly with every dress.

GIDEON: How long were you supposed to have it?

BUSBY: For one event.

GIDEON: And how long did you keep it?

BUSBY: I forget exactly. A month. Maybe two. But I returned it. That's the most important thing. I always knew it was just a loan.

GIDEON: Where did you meet to give back this necklace?

BUSBY: At her quarters. It's such a tiny little room with dreadful lighting. We chatted briefly, and then I left.

GIDEON: Did Cherish seem upset or worried about anything?

BUSBY: She wasn't her usual composed self. Her wings were ruffled, if you know what I mean. I assumed it was work stress. Demons are rather nasty creatures to deal with.

GIDEON: Was she in conflict with anyone? Did she mention any recent disputes?

BUSBY: Cherish was spending time with that demon, Maelor. I never trusted him. Slippery sort, always lurking around the edge of a party like he might hex a departing guest. I had to shoo him away several times. I told her she ought to be careful, but Cherish had a soft heart. She believed in second chances.

GIDEON: Did you witness any arguments between them?

BUSBY: No, but I got the impression Cherish was troubled by something. Perhaps she'd finally seen through Maelor.

GIDEON: You disapproved of her association with him?

BUSBY: Entirely. It was beneath her. Angels rise above corruption, not entertain it for afternoon tea. She insisted Maelor wished to make amends for his past, but I never believed it. He was drawn to her light, perhaps. Or maybe to her power. I told her he was dangerous. She only smiled and said she could handle him.

GIDEON: Do you believe Maelor wished her harm?

BUSBY: I believe he wanted something from her, and when a demon is denied, they have a way of taking what they think they deserve. Whether that was her trust, her secrets, or her life, I cannot say. But if you're looking for someone to blame, I would start there.

GIDEON: Where were you at the time of Cherish's death?

BUSBY: At my usual weekly overnight retreat. The Serenity Springs Spa. I go every week without fail for massages, mineral baths, the works. A lady has to maintain her glow. I didn't hear about Cherish until the next morning. It was quite a shock.

GIDEON: Do you recall anyone who might verify your presence there?

BUSBY: The staff, naturally. They know me well. I always book the same room and the same treatments.

GIDEON: Thank you. Is there anything else you'd like to add?

BUSBY: Only that Cherish didn't deserve such an end. She was goodness wrapped in grace. The world feels dimmer without her, though I suppose the heavens needed their perfect angel back.

FOLLOW-UP

Verify Nix Busby's visit to Serenity Springs Spa and ensure the borrowed necklace was returned.

This is a weak motive for murder, and Maelor remains the prime suspect in this investigation.

Chapter 8

After I'd sent through Nix's interview, the snow globe connection fizzled and died. No matter how many times I poked it, prodded it, or messed around with the buttons, nothing brought it back to life.

"This had better not be Cythera interfering with my only connection to the outside world," I said. "The mood she was in, she'd be spiteful enough to do this."

"We should take a break," Tansy said as she slunk out from the shadow she'd been hiding in. "I still haven't seen everything new in Badger's Haze. Come with me."

I shook my head. "You're in for a disappointment if you're expecting any luxury stores or quirky independent tearooms."

Tansy twirled in a slow circle. "It sure beats the inside of a musty old bone-filled crypt. Come on. Maybe fresh air will blow away the cobwebs and give you some inspiration. And it'll give that sad old globe time to reboot."

"I'll come with you if you tell me everything you know about Nix," I said.

"I can do better than that," Tansy replied. "I'll take you to her."

"She's still alive?" I asked.

"Not really. But I know tricks that mean we can talk to her. Follow me. This'll be so much fun."

I gave the snow globe one more kick, but then a yell from Cythera echoing from the basement sent me racing to catch up with Tansy, who was at the bottom of the stairs and heading for the main door.

The gray clouds overhead threatened more rain, but for once, I wasn't treated to a fine misting that would fuzz my fur as we walked.

"Where will we find Nix?" I asked.

"Some magic users aren't as long-lived as others," Tansy said. "We need to be creative if you want to speak to her."

"I'd be surprised if all the suspects are alive," I said. "It's fortunate most of them are angels. They have the potential to live for thousands of years."

"Demons too," Tansy said. "Unfortunately for us, Nix was an enchantress, so had an average lifespan. But she used her magic to create the best social events in Badger's Haze."

"That sounds fun," I said. "I enjoy a good party."

"Nix loved being the perfect hostess and social spinner," Tansy said. "She used to host this incredible Halloween event where everyone had to dress up as a normal person with no magic. It was hilarious. And one year she insisted everyone who had a familiar dress up as their familiar."

I stared wistfully at the path ahead. "We have a similar tradition in Crimson Cove. It takes place over the winter. Zandra dressed up as me, and then we'd chase each other through the forest."

"Oh, that sounds hilarious," Tansy said.

I slowed as I recognized the path we were taking. "Isn't this the route to your old cemetery?"

"Hush. It's definitely not my old cemetery. Not anymore," Tansy said. "Where else did you think we were going?"

"I wasn't sure," I said. "If we're heading this way, that means Nix is buried there."

"She is! But I'm happy to help you speak with her."

"You can perform necromancy?" It was an incredibly rare power, and one I'd only stumbled across a pawful of times.

"Among other things," Tansy said. "And thanks to you giving me some of your life force, I can be useful again. You want me to be useful, don't you?"

"Of course! But we're about to mess with Morticia's cemetery. She'll set Midnight on us again."

"Then we'd better hurry, hadn't we?" Tansy said with an adorable giggle. "I'll get you in and cast the magic from outside."

"You want me to go inside that spooky old cemetery alone?"

"I can't risk being trapped again," Tansy said. "For all I know, there could be an awful spell that recognizes my signature and drags me back into that crypt. I'm never going in there again. It's a hateful place."

I hesitated. Tansy was fun to be around, and I didn't want her to get in trouble. "This is a bad idea."

"Don't you want to talk to Nix and find out if she killed that charming angel?" Tansy asked.

"Why don't we use your talent to bring back Cherish?" I asked. "Get to the source. She'll be able to tell us exactly what happened that night."

"Angels respond badly to any necromantic attempt on their remains, especially when they've been dead for so long." Tansy grimaced. "I saw it done once, and the damage to the angel still haunts me. Let's leave Cherish in peace."

"Maybe we should do this another time," I said. "The angels didn't seem that suspicious of Nix."

Tansy shrugged. "It's up to you. You're the expert when solving murders. At least, that's what Sage told me."

I stared through the cemetery gates and sighed. "Let's get this over with. But I'm trusting you to be on the alert for any signs of Morticia or Midnight. They'll tear us apart if they find out we've been meddling."

"We don't want that," Tansy said with a shudder. "If I remember rightly, and I definitely do, since I've spent so long walking around here, Nix's grave is in the far-left corner near the old weeping willow. Her headstone is white marble."

"Can you get me through the magic?"

Tansy cast a spell that shimmered across the gate wards. "Off you go. Be quick. I can't hold it open for long."

I wrinkled my booping snooter but dashed into the cemetery. The air shifted the second I crossed the boundary. It was cool and unwelcoming.

I ran toward the far corner, scanning the overgrown headstones. Most had fallen into neglect, some leaning at odd angles, others cracked or shattered. A few were so weather-worn that the inscriptions had been erased.

Nix's grave was easy to find, since the overhanging weeping willow had sheltered it from the worst of the elements, so I could read her name.

I glanced around and spotted Tansy on the other side of the fence. She waved a paw at me. "Stand back. I wouldn't want to hit you with this spell."

I backed up to a safe distance and waited.

Tansy rose onto her back legs and thrust her paws forward, sending a controlled blast of magic into Nix's grave.

Nothing happened at first. Then the earth trembled. A few seconds later, a wispy figure shimmered into view, revealing a stunning, mature woman with brilliant white hair cascading in waves around her shoulders. She wore a crimson silk gown with a string of pearls around her neck. She blinked several times, confusion flickering across her elegant face.

"Oh my, that was a most unusual sensation," Nix said.

"Greetings!" I said. "I'm Juno."

Her gaze flicked to me. "You summoned me?"

"My friend did." I gestured to Tansy, who waved.

Nix looked down at her glowing form and smiled. "Divine! This was one of my favorite dresses. I wore it for the inauguration of the last king of the ogres. He was such a rogue. He tried to have his wicked way with me. Such a cheeky creature."

"It's a very nice dress," I said.

Nix smoothed an invisible crease in her gown. "Since you summoned me, you must need something. What can I do for you?"

"It's about your friend, Cherish," I said.

"Goodness! That's a name I haven't heard in some time." Nix's expression softened. "She was one of a kind, and such a hoot at my parties."

"I'm investigating what happened to her," I said. "Angel Force never solved her murder."

"Oh, it was such a dreadful business. I remember it as if it were yesterday." Nix tilted her head thoughtfully. "How long has it been?"

"Cherish has been dead for almost one hundred and fifty years," I said.

"Well now, doesn't time fly when you're no longer alive?" Nix looked at her headstone. "I still know how to enjoy myself. Just in a different way, and on a different plane of existence. You're never too old or too dead to have a party, don't you think?"

"I couldn't agree more," I said. "About Cherish. I've read the statement you gave to Angel Force after she died. Do you remember that day?"

"Like I said, it seems recent to me," Nix said. "Cherish had a way with people, much like myself. She'd find out what a person desired most and help them obtain it."

"That sounds a touch scandalous," I said.

"Not in any nefarious way! But everyone needs something," Nix said. "As long as they could give Cherish what she wanted in return, she'd help them."

"Does that include the demon she worked with, Maelor?" I asked.

Nix's face went blank for a second. "That was one thing I didn't like about Cherish's work. She brought many unsavory characters to Badger's Haze. It let down the tone. I always held this village in high esteem and wanted only the best sort of magic users to live here. That demon didn't fit the mold."

"Did you ever bring this up with Cherish and let her know you weren't happy about her working with demons?"

"We discussed it, but only in a friendly way," Nix said. "I recognized Cherish had an important job, and any demons who came to her were doing their best. Well, as much as a demon can."

"You saw her on the day she died," I said. "Did she seem troubled?"

"Not troubled, but we only spoke briefly," Nix said. "I returned a glorious silver necklace she'd so generously let me borrow for a party."

"Am I correct in thinking you didn't want to let go of that necklace?"

Nix sighed. "If you'd seen it, you'd feel the same. You'd want it fashioned into a collar and wear it proudly every day. It was lovely."

"Cherish wasn't happy you kept it for so long, was she?" I asked.

Nix waved an elegant hand in the air. "It was such a long time ago."

"You said you remember it like it was yesterday."

"I said recent, not yesterday." Nix's expression hardened. "Being gone for so long plays tricks on the mind."

"Did you argue about the necklace?"

"I... there was a small bicker, but nothing more. I kept it for too long. I'd always planned on returning it, but somehow found an excuse not to. That's not a crime, is it?"

"It depends. If you planned on keeping it for good, that's theft," I said.

Nix tutted softly. "I like pretty things. But I'm no thief. Cherish got her necklace back. I don't know why she wanted it so badly, since she rarely wore it. You should never save pretty things for a special occasion that might never happen."

"What did you do after visiting Cherish?" I asked.

"What I did every Thursday," Nix said with a wistful smile. "I had a standing appointment at the most wonderful spa, just outside Badger's Haze. At least, it used to be there. I'd book myself in and be scrubbed, rubbed, and polished to perfection. It was my weekly treat. I never deviated from it. I had to look my best because on Fridays, I hosted a party."

"After what happened to Cherish, did that party go ahead?"

"It did. We had a muted affair. Perhaps I should have canceled it," Nix said. "None of us were in the mood for fun. We turned it into a memorial. A celebration of Cherish's life, and recalled how much joy she brought to the village. She really was an extraordinary angel."

"Did Cherish ever express concerns about her safety?" I asked. "Working with demons must have come with risks."

"Cherish's confidence was extraordinary," Nix said. "She never seemed afraid, and she always believed there was goodness in everyone. I found that a touch naïve. We've all encountered truly dark souls, haven't we? But that was how she operated. And she must have been excellent at it, since she was always receiving accolades and commendations from Angel Force."

I glimpsed movement from the corner of my eye, drawing my attention to the cemetery fence. Tansy waved frantically at me.

"I can't hold this much longer," she called. "You need to wrap it up, or I'll faint!"

"Is there anyone you can think of who wanted Cherish dead?" I asked Nix.

Her image flickered, becoming translucent at the edges. "I always thought it was that demon she worked with. He was a tricky sort. Far too smooth and charming when he wanted to be, which, you know, is always a sign of trouble in a gentleman."

I nodded. We were back to Maelor as the prime suspect. "Thank you. I've already spoken to him."

"Is he still alive?" Nix arched an elegant brow. "How extraordinary."

I nodded. "He's in Badger's Haze. He was sent here to help with the investigation."

"Maelor is here?" she said. "My, my. What a turn-up for the books."

Before I could ask what Nix meant by that comment, she blinked out of sight, and the swirl of magic holding her in place dissolved with a gentle hiss.

A groan echoed from the other side of the fence. I dashed over, slipping through the gap in the wards Tansy had kept open for me.

Tansy lay flat on her back, legs sticking up in the air.

I nudged her with a paw. "Are you okay?"

She didn't move. There was no breath, no sound, no flicker of her ghostly glow. Her silence chilled me.

I nudged her again. Harder this time. "Tansy! Wake up."

Still nothing.

I gulped. Had I pushed Tansy too far, and she was dead? Again.

Chapter 9

I paused to catch my breath and crack my jaw. "Just one more street to go before we're inside, and then I'll figure out what to do with you."

I'd been ungraciously dragging Tansy by her bony tail back toward the library for almost thirty minutes. I'd failed to bring her round outside the cemetery, and didn't want to linger there longer than necessary in case Morticia or Midnight discovered what we'd been up to and enacted a vicious revenge.

"Sage will know a spell to sort you," I said, taking hold of Tansy's tail again and dragging her a few more feet.

Tansy's ghostly image was barely a whisper, her bones visible, looking like the skeletal cat I'd met inside the crypt. Using so much magic must have taken a lot out of her.

I reached the library steps and bumped Tansy up them before nudging the door open with my butt and dragging her through.

She groaned, and her skeleton shuddered.

"You're not dead!" I said. "Well, not any deader than you were the first time we met."

"What happened?" Tansy remained on her back, her bones rattling faintly.

"The magic you used to get Nix talking overwhelmed you," I said.

"It takes a lot to resurrect a life force. How did we get back to the library?" Tansy asked weakly. "Did you translocate us?"

"I did it the old-fashioned way," I said. "Can you stand? We need to get upstairs and talk to Sage. She has access to hundreds of spell books, so can get you back to normal in no time." At least I hoped she would, because my magic would only make it glitter rain or flip Tansy upside down by mistake.

Tansy flipped over and dragged herself slowly and painfully up the staircase, with me padding beside her, encouraging her every paw step of the way.

"Was it useful?" Tansy asked.

"Speaking to Nix?" I said. "She had a few things to say, but nothing surprising. Let's focus on you. I don't like the way your bones are shimmering."

It took several minutes, but we finally reached the snow globe.

"What's going on? Did someone attack Tansy?" Sage asked, her voice echoing faintly from inside the globe.

"I'm so glad the globe is working again," I said. "Tansy needs a spell to get stable. I didn't think she'd make it back here before expiring."

"Expiring? She's already dead!" Sage said. "She can't expire any more than she already has."

"There's energy still flowing through her, and we need to restore it," I said. "What spell will help her life force? Or, I suppose, her afterlife force?"

Sage leaned closer to the globe, distorting her nose. "I'll need a minute to find something."

"Actual life force," Tansy murmured. "That's the only thing that'll work for me."

I drew in a breath. "Like before?"

"That's dangerous," Sage said. "And Juno isn't powerful enough to share. She can't afford to give you any of her life force."

"Um... I don't mind," I said.

"You should mind," Sage said. "The more energy you give to someone else, the weaker you become. You're already hanging on to what magic you have by the tips of your claws, so you can't afford to lose any more."

"Would it matter if I'd done it before?" I deliberately didn't look at Sage, knowing the outrage I'd see.

Sage groaned. "I don't know why I bother. You'll do it even if I tell you not to."

"Untrue. I listen to you. Sometimes," I said.

"That was the deal you made with Tansy, wasn't it?" Sage asked. "That's why you look so faded and dull."

"Tansy knew the way out of a dangerous and life-threatening cemetery," I said. "So, we made a deal. A tiny amount of my life force in exchange for the way out."

"And that doesn't strike you as suspicious?" Sage asked.

"I'm very unsuspicious," Tansy said. "I was just bored with being trapped in one place and saw an opportunity to change my luck."

Sage muttered under her breath. "Don't say I didn't warn you."

"Take a small amount," I said to Tansy. "I feel responsible for you being like this, but I need enough energy left to solve this case."

"You'll barely notice it's gone," Tansy said as she pulled herself upright. "And thank you for bringing me back here. You could have left me beside the cemetery where I was vulnerable."

I jabbed my paw with a claw to draw blood and rested it gently on Tansy's head to allow her to siphon my life force. A chilled sensation trickled through me, numbing the tips of my ears.

"That'll do," Sage said after only a few seconds had passed.

Tansy nodded and rolled onto her paws, looking much more like her ghostly, resilient self.

"Where's Cythera?" I asked, shaking out my paw and feeling a tingle in my toe beans.

"She stomped out of here fifteen minutes ago," Sage said. "I made sure she didn't see me, so she wouldn't confiscate the snow globe."

"Maybe Cythera's gone back to the cemetery," I said. "I'll have to confront her about the real reason she's here. Lying to me will only make her even surlier."

"Let's hold off on that unfortunate conversation until we absolutely have to," Sage said. "While you were out resurrecting the dead, I researched Nix."

I hopped onto the desk, and Tansy joined me, her bones barely visible beneath her new shiny fluff. "What did you find out?"

"Nix used to be a society hostess," Sage said. "She moved to Badger's Haze when she retired, but kept holding incredible parties. They became the talk of the village. Everyone expected her to put on the best events, and she was always happy to oblige."

"She mentioned having a party just after Cherish died," I said. "They were weekly events. Where did she live before Badger's Haze?"

"Nix was married six times," Sage said. "After each divorce, she got a house, so she lived all over, but based herself in Badger's Haze after she stepped down from professional hosting."

"She was always hosting fun things," Tansy said. "Nix was a generous hostess, and she loved the gentlemen. There was talk she had several partners, even when she was married."

"Nix was honest about meeting with Cherish on the day she died," I said. "She admitted she'd returned a silver necklace she'd borrowed for too long, although she wasn't all that happy about me bringing up her social oversight. It was basically the same information she gave Angel Force."

"I also went through the statement while you were gone," Sage said. "Nix claimed she was at her usual appointment at some spa. Did that get checked? Is there anything in the file showing her alibi was followed up?"

I flipped through several old, yellowed pages. "There's a note here about the angels visiting, and there was a record in the books of Nix going to the spa. It looks like she's in the clear."

"We should still double-check," Sage said.

"How will you do that, since it was such a long time ago?" Tansy asked.

"There may be old records," Sage said. "Some businesses keep documents for decades. Some never throw them away."

I chuckled. "Do you want to go to the spa?"

"I have no desire to be pummeled by strangers and then have weird oils smeared onto my fur while whales burp in the background," Sage said. "But Vorana needs a break. With everything so stressful around here, a day at a spa with some gentle snooping on the side is just what she needs."

"Why is she so stressed?" I asked.

"Oh, you know. This and that."

"You mean this and that malfunctioning magic that I need to deal with but can't, because I'm trapped here and most of my power got absorbed by everyone living in Crimson Cove?"

Sage shrugged. "Something like that. Getting away from this place for a day will help Vorana decompress."

"Every time you mention the problems back home, I worry," I said. "I need to be there. I have to get Cythera to see sense and release me. And what's she even doing here if there are such terrible problems back in Crimson Cove?"

"You're poking around in her dead ancestor's murder," Sage said. "She wants to know what you're up to."

"Because she's guilty," Tansy whispered. "I think the big, grumpy angel who stamps and snarls is the killer."

"Do you really think an angel did this?" I asked.

Tansy nodded. "It's got to be Cythera. She's terrifying."

"It would need to be someone as powerful as Cythera," I mused. "There are few supernatural beings who can destroy an angel. That's why they make up the backbone of law enforcement."

Tansy's eyes widened. "Do you think it was her? Have I solved this crime? Will you confront Cythera? She needs to be confronted. She seems to me like a terrible angel."

"It is shocking. But no, I don't think you've solved it. And I value my life too much to do that," I said. "But I must question Cythera about Cherish without her whacking me too hard with a wing."

"Just not right now," Sage said.

"But soon," I replied. "If things are getting bad in Crimson Cove, then time isn't on our side. You send Vorana to the spa to see what information she can find in any historical records."

"I'll book her in for a massage," Sage said. "Something top to toe."

"Sounds good," I said. "And I'll dig into the next suspect."

"Who are you choosing?" Tansy asked.

I looked at the list. I'd have to move on to the angel suspects soon, which meant getting Cythera involved, something I looked forward to about as much as having my claws clipped.

"We have one more suspect who used to live here. Maybe he still does," I said. "Sage, I'm sending you Yahir Hallow's interview."

"I'm ready when you are," Sage said.

I fiddled with the globe, which made a rude noise, fizzled for a few seconds, and then sent the paperwork.

ANGEL FORCE INTERVIEW TRANSCRIPT

Case file: #32-1875
Conducted by: Angel Gideon
Interviewee: Yahir Hallow

GIDEON: Mr. Hallow, I appreciate your willingness to meet at short notice.
HALLOW: Of course. And my apologies that we had to meet away from my home. The renovations are taking much longer than planned, and there's too much noise and dust to deal with.
GIDEON: That must be frustrating.
HALLOW: Indeed. My work keeps me busy, so the delay is unwelcome. Anyway, how may I assist you?
GIDEON: You're aware of Cherish's death?
HALLOW: I am. It's a sad business. I can scarcely believe she's gone.
GIDEON: You knew the deceased well?

HALLOW: We worked together on preservation and cataloguing projects. Cherish would often acquire items of significance when negotiating with demons. I would ensure they were safe and suitably maintained.

GIDEON: Having spoken to some of your colleagues, there was mention of your relationship being strained. There were disagreements over how certain relics should be used.

HALLOW: Those were intellectual disputes, nothing more. When cataloging sacred artifacts, there are usually differences of opinion. Everyone is suddenly an expert.

GIDEON: Do you consider yourself an expert on halo fragments? Did you know about them?

HALLOW: Cherish mentioned them, though I never saw the objects. Such items would require careful handling. If a halo is damaged, the power within becomes unstable.

GIDEON: Cherish didn't ask you to catalog the items?

HALLOW: No. Perhaps she planned to, but then this tragedy happened. Do you want me to look at them?

GIDEON: Not at this time. The fragments are evidence in the investigation.

HALLOW: I am at your disposal

whenever you need an expert eye.

GIDEON: I appreciate that. Focusing on the night Cherish died, where were you when she fell from the bell tower?

HALLOW: Walking. I often stroll through the lanes.

GIDEON: Near the bell tower?

HALLOW: Yes. It's a favorite walk. Near the tower, the cemetery guardian stores the oldest headstones that have fallen into disrepair or needed removing because they became unsafe. I enjoy exploring them.

GIDEON: So late?

HALLOW: I often walk late in the evening. It helps to calm my mind so I sleep more easily.

GIDEON: Did anyone see you during this walk?

HALLOW: I cannot say. I passed a cart on the road, but it was dark and the driver paid me no notice. I heard a noise. It sounded like something heavy hit the ground, but I didn't stop to see what it was.

GIDEON: And what time did you return home?

HALLOW: Close to midnight, perhaps a little after. I retired at once.

GIDEON: Do you live with anyone who can confirm that?

HALLOW: You may think this sad, but my work is my only passion.

My books cannot be my alibi, but I assure you, I don't need one. I had a professional relationship with Cherish. We respected each other. I'd never wish her harm.

GIDEON: Did Cherish ever express fear or mistrust toward anyone in the weeks before her death?

HALLOW: Not to me, but Cherish dealt with difficult characters and must have carried many secrets, especially given her dealings with so many demons. Some said one in particular, Maelor, had taken too keen an interest in her affairs.

GIDEON: You knew this demon?

HALLOW: I was aware he had moved to Badger's Haze and was working with Cherish. I had nothing to do with that side of her work, though.

GIDEON: Cherish never mentioned him?

HALLOW: We spoke only of relics.

GIDEON: Thank you. That will be all for now.

HALLOW: Of course. I'm always willing to assist. This is a sad loss for our little community.

FOLLOW UP

Speak to more of Hallow's colleagues in the Relics division to gauge the extent of the disputes between Hallow and Cherish.

This is a limited motive for wanting Cherish dead, although there is no alibi.

The demon Maelor remains the prime suspect.

Chapter 10

"Did the angels do any follow-up after they interviewed Yahir?" Sage asked.

I spent a minute checking the file. "Not that I can see."

"Maybe they talked to more of his colleagues and realized he was a dead end," Sage said.

"He could have lied about his interest in the halo fragments," I said. "He could be a sneaky, covetous relic historian who saw something shiny and wanted it. Those fragments would have huge power."

"I suppose Yahir's another one you'll need to dig up," Sage said. "Or is he alive?"

"Definitely dead." Tansy perched on top of a stack of books. "Yahir was incinerated a long time ago."

"You mean cremated," I said.

"No, incinerated," Tansy repeated. "His house caught fire while he was inside. He never made it out."

"What a dreadful way to go," Sage murmured.

"It's no surprise the place went up so fast. Yahir was a hoarder. He loved anything old, and he had an addiction to books. Every space had a book on it.

All highly flammable." Tansy hopped off the books and floated to the floor. "He had an entire room set aside for ancient parchments. Apparently, that was where the blaze started. The fire was put out before it destroyed all the rooms, but Yahir didn't stand a chance."

"We may still be able to talk to him," I said. "Tansy, were his ashes scattered around here?"

"Yes! Well, I think they got most of him once the fire was out," she said. "He has a plot in the old cemetery."

I groaned. "Not there again."

"It's not so bad," Tansy said. "Well, no, that's untrue. It's a terrible place, but my bad memories are fading, so I already think of it a little more fondly. I may even come in with you this time."

"You'll get all sorts of weird coming through a spell if you don't know what Yahir's ashes were contaminated with," Sage warned. "If he messed with relics and ancient parchments, it could get tricky."

"I don't think it'll be terrible, although I didn't see the collection process," Tansy said. "I know the angels used magic to recover what was left of Yahir. There were teeth to give them a starting point."

"Yahir could be a useful source of information. Do you remember if he had any issues with Cherish?" I asked Tansy.

She twitched her nose from side to side. "I don't know for sure. He was obsessed with his work. He'd get so excited when he found a relic and would talk anyone's ears off about it. I guess he'd have wanted to talk to Cherish. Maybe that annoyed her."

"He mentioned the halo fragments in his statement," I said.

"Oh yes," Tansy replied. "He talked about setting up an exhibition based on what he believed was an original angel halo."

Sage whistled. "I can't see that being true. Something that powerful and rare would be a target. Do you think he approached Cherish with the idea, and she turned him down?"

"Maybe. Angel Force would have wanted input," I said. "An original relic like that would hold tremendous amounts of power. It would be dangerous in the wrong hands."

"I don't think it was proven to be an original halo," Tansy said. "I'm not surprised. It seems so unlikely. A few people even called Yahir a charlatan and said he was trying to sell a relic as something else to give him a moment of fame."

"Let's talk to Yahir," I said. "Tansy, can you show me where he is?"

"Of course. I could walk that cemetery in my sleep with my eyes closed. I frequently did when I was bored," she said. "There's an area set aside for urn burials. Follow me. We'll soon get our crispy friend talking."

"Such disrespect for the dead," Sage muttered. "While you're gone, I'll look into Yahir's background and see just how successful he really was."

We said our goodbyes, and I left the library with Tansy. It was getting late, and the moon was peeking out from behind a bank of ominous yellow clouds. Surely, it wasn't about to snow!

"This is becoming a regular thing," I said to Tansy.

"Going back to my terrible prison?"

I nodded. "There's something about that place that makes my toe beans tingle."

She glanced at me. "You know who's buried there, don't you?"

"I know little about the old cemetery," I said. "I keep away from cemeteries unless absolutely necessary. What's so bad about this one?"

Tansy slowed. "It was never an official cemetery. People started using it to lay their dead to rest after the incident in the haunted house."

"What incident? And what haunted house?"

"I'm wooly on the details, since it was long before my time," Tansy said. "The rumors go that one of the first buildings put up in Badger's Haze was home to a wicked old witch. She thrived on dark magic and used more and more of it until everyone living nearby was terrified."

"Did the locals make a plan to stop her?" I asked.

Tansy nodded. "They needed to make sure this crooked old magic user couldn't hurt anyone else ever again."

"What did they do to her?"

"They paid a dragon to knock down her house and eat her!" Tansy said. "However, things didn't go as planned. She was incredibly powerful, and although the dragon ate her, he couldn't keep her down. He tried for days, but she kept fighting, even though he'd chewed her up."

"What did the dragon do?"

"He dug a deep hole and spat her into it. Then he blasted dragon fire all over her and sealed her in."

"And that's how the cemetery began?"

"Got it in one."

"But why would people want their dearly departed anywhere near such a twisted old magic user?" I asked.

"It's not just any dead buried there," Tansy said. "That old crone unleashed something in Badger's Haze, and it slowly seeped through the town, affecting the vulnerable."

"Is that when things started to go wrong for the village?"

"Could be." Tansy glanced around. "And when other people misbehaved, they were dealt with and sealed away in the old cemetery, too."

I stopped as we reached the gate. "Does that mean you were sealed here because you used dark magic?"

"Oh, no. I'm a special case. Let's meet Yahir, shall we?"

"You're coming in with me?"

"Why not? I like to live dangerously. Besides, Yahir's ashes will need careful containment so he doesn't float away."

I lingered behind Tansy. What had she done to deserve being put in an old cemetery full of dark, twisted magic users?

"Keep up," she called. "I'll only be able to use the spell for a short time, unless you want to give me even more of your life force. And I don't think your grumpy friend would appreciate you doing that. You know, I don't think Sage likes me."

"She often doesn't like me, too." I walked past the rows of crooked headstones and crumbling mausoleums and stopped on the edge of a patch of brown grass. The landscaping looked dead. The grass was crispy, and the soil was dry, despite the never-ending drizzle.

"He's over here," Tansy said, gesturing for me to follow her.

I stepped tentatively onto the grass and shuddered. Everything about this place felt wrong, so I skipped the rest of the way, stopping to perch on the edge of a small, crooked grave marker with a weathered headstone leaning back precariously.

"I'll give you three minutes to talk to Yahir," Tansy said. She was already sparking magic between her paws. "Any longer and you'll be dragging me back to the library again."

"Got it. I'll keep it brief," I said. "Let's hope Yahir behaves."

Tansy cast the magic, and it flooded across the headstone. There was a trembling beneath our paws, and a few seconds later, a swirl of ash and dust rose through a tiny hole in the grave.

The cloud took a few seconds to form, but eventually, it shaped into a man sitting cross-legged, hunched over with his head down.

"Greetings! I'm Juno, and this is Tansy," I said. "I'm looking for Yahir Hallow. Would that be you?"

The grainy image shifted and then coughed. "What do you want?"

I explained why I was there. By the time I'd finished, his form had solidified, and he looked at me with sharp interest.

"I was never able to finish my work," Yahir said. "Those angels were always stopping me. They keep secrets, you know."

"I've worked with Angel Force for years," I said. "They're not as pure as they like everyone to believe."

Yahir grunted. "Did any of my belongings survive the fire? I often think about my collection."

"Most of the rooms survived," Tansy said. "There must have been smoke damage, though. I heard your belongings were cleared out."

Yahir's image disintegrated for a second before reforming. "Cleared out! They stole them! Those deceitful angels took my valuables. They must have sold them to pay for some pointless efficiency measures."

"Cherish was working with fragments of angel halo shortly before she died," I said. "Do you remember that?"

"Halo fragments! Yes, I recall something about those. But she was only ever interested in dealing with dodgy types," Yahir said. "I asked her questions about it, but she didn't want me involved. It was a shame. I'm an expert. Well, I was. It was her loss. Selfish to keep something like that, when so many could have enjoyed it."

"How well did you know Cherish?" I asked.

"Well enough to know she had no interest in preserving history," Yahir said. "She just kept talking about redemption, giving people a chance to make themselves better, and all that nonsense. I told her it would make more sense to focus on history and learn from mistakes. That would give people a better education. But she wasn't for turning, no matter what I said."

"That must have frustrated you," I said.

"It frustrated me that Cherish let all those demons into Badger's Haze," Yahir said. "We all know never to trust a demon. Some of them have light fingers! Most of them. There was an increase in crime when she opened her office here. And can you imagine what a demon would do if they ever got their claws into a piece of angel halo?"

"I doubt it would be a happy ending," I said.

"You've got that right. I paid for extra protection wards around my collection, just to be sure no sneaky demon would steal anything."

"From what you've said, you weren't Cherish's biggest fan," I said.

"Now look here, I know what you're digging into, and there's no use in pointing the finger at me," Yahir said.

"Cats don't have fingers," Tansy said.

"You know what I mean! I told Angel Force everything of value, and nothing's changed."

"Could you remind me of your alibi that night?" I asked.

"It sounds like you've read the file information, although I'm unable to fathom why they put you in charge, so you already know it," Yahir said. "I told the angel who spoke to me that I was near the tower when everything went wrong. I even heard a thud, and that could have been Cherish falling, but I wasn't there to witness it."

"You didn't investigate?"

"And get myself in trouble with a demon?" Yahir said. "I shouldn't have been out, but my mind was restless, so I knew I shouldn't sleep. And I enjoy moonlight headstone rubbing."

"What's that?" I asked.

"You rest paper over the stone and rub it with charcoal to get an impression of the words and images. It's a fascinating hobby," Yahir said. "I even had a small exhibition of my rubbings. Old stonework is stunning and so full of hints of the past."

"Did you do any rubbings that night?" I asked.

"No. I left my charcoal behind, which was a pity."

"If you'd been at the tower, you may have seen Cherish's attacker," Tansy said.

"I'm a man of intellect, not attack. I would have been of no value in such a deadly situation." Yahir made a show of straightening his cuffs. "I didn't like the work Cherish did, but I am sorry for what happened to her. Do you know what shocked me? When that demon she spent so much time with wasn't arrested."

"Do you remember the demon's name?" I asked.

"Maelor. He was a shifty one." Yahir's image flickered, and I looked over to see Tansy shaking.

"Can you hold on a moment longer?" I asked.

She nodded. "Hurry!"

"Maelor turned on his own kind," Yahir said. "There's nothing more deceitful than that. I didn't believe a word that came out of that criminal's mouth."

"You think Maelor killed Cherish?" I said.

"Who else? I remember the rumors saying he heard someone in the bell tower arguing with Cherish. But there was no evidence of that. It had to be him, but he got away with it. Disgraceful!"

"Did you see anyone running from the bell tower?" I asked.

"No, I saw nothing. Now, about what's left of my collection. I want it—" Yahir disintegrated into ash and sank into the dirt.

Tansy was shaking and panting but still conscious as the spell faded.

"Did you get what you needed?" she asked. "Sorry, but I couldn't hold the spell any longer."

"I think so," I said. "Everyone is pointing a finger at Maelor."

"Well, I don't want to follow the crowd, but Maelor is a devious demon," Tansy said. "Maybe Angel Force was more cautious back then, because they believed he had valuable information and they didn't want to lose an important informant."

"I'm not cautious, and he's not helping me," I said. "Perhaps we need to look again at Maelor."

Tansy's gaze cut over my shoulder, and her eyes widened.

I turned and spotted the ground frosting over as Morticia stomped toward me. I turned back to Tansy to tell her to hide, but she'd already vanished. Clever cat.

I dodged behind Yahir's headstone, giving myself a second to make a plan. But the frost was approaching fast, and with it, the malevolently icy tang of Morticia's magic.

If I ran as fast as I could, maybe I could get to the fence in time. Tansy would be watching. She'd help me get through the wards. It was my only hope because there was no way I'd be able to fight Morticia and come out on the other side alive.

I darted toward the fence, but only made it a dozen paw-steps before I was lifted off the ground by my tail. I slashed my murder mittens through the air, but it was no use.

Morticia flipped me around, grabbed me by the scruff, and held me up to her face, her eyes sparking with malice and her teeth bared.

I gulped. There was no way I was getting out of this in one piece.

Chapter 11

My attempts to twist out of Morticia's punishing hold only made my neck hurt. "Before you destroy me, I'd like you to write a note and pass it to my wonderful witch, Zandra Crypt."

Morticia glowered at me, her hair flying around in an unnatural wind. "If you truly are about to draw your final breath, what would the message be?"

It took me a moment to regain control of my panic. "I'm sorry I let her down. I thought I was helping, but by giving away my powers to others, I've separated us."

"Would you have done it if you'd known the outcome?" Morticia asked.

I hesitated. As much as I wanted to be with Zandra, giving away my magic had helped so many friends I knew I'd have in my life forever. But what a cost! Being separated from my bonded witch for so long was a form of slow torture.

"I'd do it again, even though it hurts every day to be without Zandra," I said. "Crimson Cove is worthy of saving."

Morticia's mouth twisted to the side in a sort of smile. "It's your lucky night. I'm not killing you."

I peered at her in surprise. "Even though I keep breaking into your cemeteries and disturbing your dead?"

"Under any other circumstances, you'd be toast. But we need to talk about Cherish." She dropped me into the dirt. "Follow me."

Morticia strode away without looking over her shoulder, heading toward a large mausoleum with a hunched stone gnome perched on top. She touched the gnome's foot, and a door opened. Without hesitation, she stepped into the darkness beyond.

As tempting as it was to run the other way, curiosity got the better of me. Why did Morticia want to talk about Cherish? And why hadn't she blasted me into oblivion? Maybe her date had gone better than expected.

I entered the gloomy passageway, barely able to see her outline ahead.

"Don't dawdle," Morticia called. "There are things in here that would happily eat you as a midnight snack."

I hurried along, dodging cobwebs and broken stone. "Where are we going?"

"You'll find out if you can keep up and don't get eaten," Morticia said.

I ran until I was almost standing on her trailing hem. We walked for ten minutes in silence until the floor sloped slightly up. Morticia slowed, and a small light flickered to life. There was a scrape of stone against stone, and a door slid open.

We continued along another short passage, through another door, and then into a large circular room lit by a variety of softly glowing purple lamps. It was a cozily messy space with comfortable chairs, cushions, and blankets scattered about, with an earthy scent in the air.

"Is this part of your home?" I asked.

"I prefer to call it my lair," Morticia said. She made herself a drink and sat in a high-backed chair, not offering me anything, so I remained standing, feeling as though I was about to be interrogated.

Morticia stared at me in silence for several long, uncomfortable minutes before setting down her glass. "How are you progressing with the case?"

"I'm surprised you know anything about it," I said.

"Midnight."

That was all she needed to say. Midnight was everywhere. Her eyes and ears in every corner of this cursed village.

"Of course," I said. "Well, I'm getting through the suspects. May I ask why you have an interest?"

Her gaze slid to the side. "I liked Cherish. She was the only person in the last hundred-odd years I'd call a friend."

I wasn't sure I could hide my surprise, so I took a few seconds to settle myself on the soft rug. "What did you like about her?"

"She was tolerant of everyone and never passed judgment until she truly knew a person," Morticia said. "Most form an opinion after only seconds, but that's no way to understand a soul."

"I don't disagree," I said. "That's why Cherish thrived working with demons. An unusual angel, indeed."

"She ensured everyone got at least a second chance at redemption," Morticia said. "Although some of the stories she told me about her work were hair-raising."

"You spent time together?" I asked.

"We did." Morticia glared at me. "I want her killer punished. The way Angel Force handled things when she was shoved out of the bell tower was an embarrassing joke."

"You told them that?"

"I demanded they open an inquiry into why the case was never solved."

"There's no note of an inquiry in the cold case file," I said.

"That's because they ignored me. They even tried to have me removed from Badger's Haze because I caused a stink. They had the nerve to go to the top of the Cemetery Guardian Guild and inform on me. As if that would accomplish anything." Morticia snorted. "I'm one of the best cemetery guardians ever to exist. You don't stay in a place like this and deal with centuries of unrest without being able to handle yourself."

"But you still didn't get your inquiry into why the case wasn't solved?"

Morticia hissed. "Angel Force tied things up in so much bureaucracy that by the time I sliced through it, the leads were cold. The angels involved in the case had been conveniently moved to places where they were almost impossible to reach. And don't think I didn't try."

"Why would that be?" I asked. "Unless an angel was involved in what happened to Cherish, there'd be no reason to stop them from assisting in solving the crime."

"Exactly my point." Morticia jabbed a finger at me. "It had to be an angel. It would take another angel to destroy Cherish."

I tilted my head from side to side. "There are other magic users who could achieve it and a few spells that would do the job, but you're right. I was thinking the same thing. It wouldn't be your average everyday magic user who committed this crime."

"Cherish had power," Morticia said. "It was the only reason she survived in her job. Some of the demons she worked with were bluffing when they said they wanted to assist. They thought they could infiltrate the angels and cause chaos. Cherish was always there to bring them down. She believed in redemption and second chances, but if someone crossed her, she destroyed them."

"She sounds like a fascinating character," I said. "I wish I'd known her when she was alive."

"She was different from the other angels, which meant she didn't fit in," Morticia said. "They only kept her around because she got a job done that none of the others would touch. She saved a lot of lives."

"I imagine her work improved Angel Force's conviction rate, too," I said.

"Yep. They are always obsessed with meeting their targets," Morticia smirked, but it quickly faded. "Cherish deserved better. She got a lousy deal, and I want that fixed."

"That's what I'm working toward."

"You'd better make it happen," Morticia said darkly, "because the list of misdeeds against you grows longer every day."

I shuffled my position on the rug. "I can't imagine what you're referring to."

"Don't think you'll get away with sneaking into my place and stealing Cherish's file."

"Ah! You know about that?"

"I know about everyone who trespasses in my space," Morticia said.

"It was for the greater good," I replied.

"Which is why you're still breathing," Morticia said. "For now."

"Forever, I hope."

Morticia grunted. "There's more you need to know about Cherish. She was looking into something. Not just misbehaving demons that caused trouble for Angel Force, but an issue right here in Badger's Haze."

"Does this have to do with the curse?" I asked.

Morticia nodded. "I'd say I'm one of the oldest residents in the village. I was sent here when the old cemetery was still active. It had been kicking out abnormal energy signatures, and I had to figure out what was going on."

"I've learned more about that cemetery," I said. "I know its origins."

"The witch from the haunted house, you mean?" Morticia asked. "There were traces of her magic lingering in the soil, which fed other corpses, but that I could handle. She wasn't the problem."

"Who was?"

"People from outside of Badger's Haze had been creeping in and using the edges of the cemetery to dispose of troublesome types no one wanted near them."

"That sounds worrying," I said.

"They were destroying their enemies and then dumping their problems here," Morticia said. "I need to know every magical signature that goes into the ground, or I can't control it or absorb what's left of the power. That's when the problem started."

"Village gossip claims someone cursed or hexed Badger's Haze," I said. "But did Cherish figure out it was someone hidden in the cemetery?"

"If I had to wager my fortune, I'd say there's something nasty in that old cemetery, and it's been seeping across the village for a long time. That was part of the reason I insisted it be closed and contained by magical wards. I thought it would be enough to stop the problem growing, but by then it was too late."

"The corrupted magic was bothering everybody," I said.

"Mainly the weak-willed. Cherish noticed," Morticia said. "She didn't always live here. She would come and go, bringing demons to stay because this place was more welcoming than most. But one night, I took her to the old cemetery. She spent hours there, walking around, casting spells. When she was done, she said she was worried and wanted to figure out the problem. Cherish was a fixer. She believed there was a solution to every issue."

"There usually is, if you're willing to put in the time and effort," I said.

"You sound just like her," Morticia replied with an appraising look.

"I'll take that as a compliment."

"Don't. After all, she's dead, and you've had plenty of near misses since you arrived."

"How close do you think Cherish was to solving the mystery?" I asked.

Morticia shrugged. "Close enough to get herself killed."

"You think her murder had to do with the cemetery, and not the demon she was working with when she died?"

"That's for you to figure out," Morticia said.

Excitement bubbled inside me. "If Cherish came close to solving the puzzle of why this village is in ruins, I could finish what she started and help everyone here."

"That's a reach too far," Morticia said. "If Cherish failed to do it, there's no way you will."

"You think I'm incapable?" I asked.

"You may have achieved it when you had all your powers." Morticia narrowed her eyes. "When you were a demigoddess."

I sucked in a breath. "You've done your research. How did you find out?"

"I have my sources. You don't need to know who they are," Morticia said. "But you've not made it a secret that you gave away your magic to help others. That leaves you without the abilities you once had to solve this mystery."

"I've already solved two cases with barely any magic," I said. "And my powers are growing."

"I've heard about your pathetic attempts to botch together spells." Morticia smirked again. "Face facts. This is beyond you."

I twitched my booping snooter, rattled by her confident belief in my lack of ability. "I'll prove you wrong."

Morticia considered me before draining her glass. "Let's even the odds in your favor, since I want answers. I'll give you a free pass to the cemeteries, so you won't have to worry about me chasing you out. In return, you solve Cherish's murder and bring her killer to justice."

"That would be incredibly helpful," I said. "What's the catch?"

"The catch is, if you fail, you'll find yourself in big trouble. Nothing and nobody will stop me from getting rid of you." Morticia passed a finger across her throat.

I forced a laugh, but I could tell Morticia wasn't joking. "I won't let you down."

"Then we have a deal." Morticia nodded. "We're done here. Get lost."

"Before I do, the next stage in this case will be tricky," I said. "There were angels questioned at the time of Cherish's death. Angel Force will block me from getting to them."

"Just like they blocked me," Morticia said, leaning back in her seat. "You need to talk to Verity, Lumiel, and Aurek, don't you?"

"I do. Do you remember them being around at the time of Cherish's murder?"

"They were always hanging around. And you're right. Once Angel Force gets wind that you want to question one of their own, they'll flare their wings and block you at every turn."

"I have contacts in Angel Force who may help," I said, "but it could take time before we can access those angels."

"And the suspects you've spoken to so far haven't proved conclusive?" Morticia asked.

"Everyone's pointing toward Maelor, and I don't disagree that he's an obvious suspect."

"But he's too obvious," Morticia finished for me. "I thought the same when it all went down. Maelor's a nothing demon. His powers are limited. He wouldn't have been able to hurt Cherish, and if he'd tried, she'd have crushed him like a fly."

"Which leads me back to the angel suspects," I said.

Morticia stood and left the room. She returned a moment later, holding a large white feather.

"I take it that's not for me to play with?" I asked.

"I plucked this from an idiot angel who got too close and was far too obnoxious for his own good," Morticia said.

I peered at the feather. "What can you use it for?"

Morticia bared her teeth. "How about we summon ourselves an angel to interrogate?"

Chapter 12

"You may not have much magic, but you have luck on your side." Sage was shaking her head as I finished telling her and Tansy about my encounter with Morticia.

"I thought you were done for," Tansy said. "I'm sorry I didn't help, but I panicked and fled back here as fast as I could."

"I told you to run," I said. "I'm glad Morticia didn't catch you."

"Because you charmed her into keeping you alive," Tansy said.

"I wish that were true. Morticia is helping because she wants something out of this," I said.

"Probably your soul and each one of those toe beans to stir into a spell," Sage said. "You can't trust her to do the right thing."

"I didn't say I trusted her," I replied. "But she was genuine. Even though she was raging about the angels and bubbling over with anger, I got a glimpse of Morticia's softer side."

"Cemetery guardians can't afford to have soft sides," Sage said. "And if Morticia is so intent on helping, why hasn't she summoned one of the angel suspects yet?"

"She said it would take up to twenty-four hours before the spell was strong enough," I said. "It takes a lot of juice to drag an angel into Badger's Haze."

"We should use the contacts we have," Sage said. "I'll ask Finn to get on the case."

"I considered that, but it'll take too long and put Finn in danger," I said. "He does what he can, but he hasn't got contacts everywhere."

"He's got some shady ones, though," Sage said. "And it's better it takes more time than to deal with a cemetery guardian who doesn't play fair."

"All Morticia wants is justice for Cherish. Just like us."

Sage scowled. "Watch your back around Morticia."

"I do. And my front. And my sides," I said. "So long as we solve this case, I have nothing to worry about."

"That's no small task," Sage said. "Just don't get killed."

"How's it going with Vorana?" I asked. "Has she been to the spa yet?"

"She's booked in. She'll poke around and let me know if she finds anything useful to help confirm Nix's spa alibi."

"While we wait for Morticia's brew to be ready, let's review another statement." I pulled out the paper, which was disintegrating with age, pressed a few buttons on the snow globe, and hoped the content wouldn't crumble before Sage read it.

ANGEL FORCE INTERVIEW TRANSCRIPT

Case file: #32-1875

Conducted by: Angel Gideon
Interviewee: Angel Verity

GIDEON: I appreciate your cooperation. I understand this is a difficult time for you.
VERITY: It is. Cherish was my cousin, and she was kind enough to take me under her wing when I joined Angel Force. I never thought I'd be giving a statement about her death.
GIDEON: You were training under her, were you not?
VERITY: Yes. I'd been assigned to shadow her for three months.
GIDEON: Tell me about the day she died. Did you see her?
VERITY: Only briefly after I'd eaten. She was busy and told me to finish reviewing the case files she'd given me. Cherish had information about two demons who were considering working with her, but wanted to run a background check and speak to contacts before taking things further.
GIDEON: Did Cherish mention where she was going or who she intended to meet?

VERITY: She said that she needed to speak to an old friend, which I took to mean another informer. Cherish was careful with her words, so as not to reveal too much and get her informants in trouble.

GIDEON: Understandable. What about any problems she was having with her work?

VERITY: Nothing comes to mind.

GIDEON: Was she worried about anyone? Did she mention the names of any magic users she was concerned about?

VERITY: Nothing like that. Although Cherish spent a lot of time with her current informer. Maelor.

GIDEON: What was your opinion of him?

VERITY: He was shifty. Cherish didn't want me working directly with the demons, so I had limited exposure to him, but he was always around.

GIDEON: Did he do anything to concern you? Act inappropriately?

VERITY: No. But I was always cautious of him. I wish Cherish had been more cautious. She'd still be alive.

GIDEON: You lodged together, I believe?

VERITY: We shared a house provided by Angel Force. My room was next to hers.

GIDEON: And on the night of her death, where were you?

VERITY: In my room, reading through the records she'd assigned me. Around half-past eleven, Mr. Trenton, our housing manager, knocked on my door to see if I'd like a drink before he closed the kitchen. I declined.

GIDEON: Did you hear your cousin return at any point during the evening?

VERITY: No. I fell asleep not long after Mr. Trenton checked on me. Someone from Angel Force woke me early the next morning to tell me what had happened. This is terrible. Is it really true?

GIDEON: I'm afraid so, and I'm sorry for your loss. You've conducted yourself admirably under distressing circumstances.

VERITY: Thank you. The world already feels dimmer without her in it. Is there anything I can do to help find who did this?

GIDEON: That will be all for now. I may contact you again should we require further details, though I don't expect that will be necessary.

VERITY: I understand. Please find whoever did this.

FOLLOW UP

Verify Lodging Manager's Account, and confirm Mr. Trenton's statement regarding Verity's presence in her quarters at approximately 11:30 p.m.

At this stage, no further action is required. Verity's account is consistent with the corroborated testimony. We consider the subject cooperative and unlikely to be involved.

Chapter 13

After some much-needed sleep, snacks, and grooming, we were back in the thick of the suspect pile bright and early the next day.

"I'm deeply unimpressed with how apathetic Angel Force were once again," Sage said. "It's like they weren't even trying to dig for motives."

Tansy rolled onto her back. "They went easy on Verity. I remember her. She was sweet. Jumpy, though. She definitely looked up to Cherish."

"Did anyone bother to check if Verity was even where she said she was at the time of the murder?" Sage asked.

I rifled through the file. "There was a check done with Mr. Trenton."

"Wonders will never cease. What did he say?" Sage asked.

"He looked in on Verity, just as she said," I said.

"It would have been easy for Verity to sneak out and go to the bell tower," Sage said.

"What's the address of the housing they were in?" Tansy asked.

I reeled it off.

Tansy closed her eyes and scrunched up her face. "That's about a five-minute walk from the bell tower."

"There you go! It would have been easy for Cherish to get there and back with nobody noticing," Sage said.

"She could even have flown," I said. "It would have taken minutes."

"While I read the statement, I also looked into Verity's background," Sage said. "That whole family had a reputation for excellence."

"Had?" I asked.

"Their standing has gone downhill faster than a no-legged cauldron on a slope," Sage said. "Many of them went into law enforcement, some went into the courts, and a few sat on various guild boards. When they spoke, people listened."

"But then Cherish got involved with demons," I said, "and things went wrong?"

Sage nodded. "Ever since Cherish took on the role of working within demonic circles, the family's reputation declined. The more she helped the demons, the worse it got."

"And even though they claim not to be, angels can be full of pride," I said. "It must have struck a blow to the family to have their name smeared with demon excrement."

"Yuck. That makes me want to take a bath," Tansy said.

"Demons are often stinky," I agreed. "It gives Verity a powerful motive for wanting Cherish dead."

"Yet Angel Force let her off without so much as a simple grilling and zero follow-up," Sage said.

"Were they covering for one of their own?" I pondered. "With Cherish dead, the family could rebuild its reputation."

A blast of icy wind shot through the library, and Midnight flickered into view. He looked around before spotting me. "Morticia's spell is ready. Don't keep her waiting."

"I've got to go. Good work, Sage." I followed Midnight out of the library and into the gloomy street.

"I saw something shocking earlier," Midnight said.

"Not more trouble in the old cemetery?" I asked.

"Morticia smiled! It always makes me nervous when she's smiling."

I chuckled. "It's because I'm helping her friend."

"She mentioned you'd made a deal." Midnight slid a glance at me. "Just watch yourself with Morticia's deals. Mess up and you're dead."

"I know what I'm doing," I said. "I just need to find out who murdered Cherish. And maybe figure out a way for Badger's Haze to recover."

"Don't get too cocky," Midnight warned. "You've solved two cases. That doesn't make you an expert."

"Maybe I've only solved two cases in Badger's Haze," I said, "but you should see my track record in Crimson Cove. I've got angels lining up to give me medals for my hard work."

Midnight snorted a laugh. "Yeah, good one. That's when they're not slinging you into cursed villages and telling you to abandon all hope."

"About that," I said. "Morticia thinks Cherish was onto something big. Something to do with why this village has been hexed and abandoned by the angels. Do you know anything about that?"

"Maybe."

"Are you willing to share?"

"Will you meddle if I do?"

"I'm already meddling."

"And sinking into trouble with every paw step, but it's your funeral."

"I hope you wear something colorful when the time comes to mourn me."

"All I know," Midnight said, "is that one day this place was fine. The stores were flourishing, people were happy, and the magic behaved. Then, this creeping gloom spread everywhere. It happened so slowly that we barely noticed what was going on until it was too late. By then, none of us had the energy or desire to change things."

"Morticia said it was creeping out of the old cemetery," I said. "Someone buried something there they shouldn't have, and it's causing problems for the whole village."

"I've heard her talk about that," Midnight said. "But unless we're digging up the entire cemetery and cleansing each unauthorized burial, body by body, bone by bone, there's nothing we can do."

"Why haven't you tried that?" I asked. "Sure, it would take time, but you'd clear the problem."

"You've been inside the cemetery," Midnight said. "It's a deadly place to linger. The things buried around the edges are full of ill intent. Stay too long, and it infects you. There's no way we could cover all that ground without destroying ourselves."

"We could try," I said.

Midnight slowed as we reached the gates of the old cemetery. "You're planning on sticking around long enough to make that happen, I suppose?"

I drew in a breath. Badger's Haze was a temporary base. I wasn't putting down roots here.

"Thought not," Midnight said. "The second you can, you'll be out of here, and I don't blame you. I'd follow if I could, but I go where Morticia goes. So, I'm stuck here."

"Maybe you could suggest a move to Morticia," I said. "You could come to Crimson Cove."

"And do what?" Midnight flicked his tail toward the gate. "Come on. Morticia's waiting, and you never want to keep her waiting."

"What happens if I do?"

Midnight grimaced. "You don't want to find out."

Chapter 14

When we entered Morticia's lair, as she so charmingly called it, the place smelled of burning herbs. A small cauldron bubbled in one corner, steam rising off it in curling wisps.

"Are you ready?" Morticia asked, without preamble.

"Let's get the angel here," I said. "How long do I have?"

"As long as you need. The spell will keep the angel here for as long as the feather remains floating in the cauldron."

"Then dip it in," I said.

Morticia held the feather over the cauldron. "Who am I dragging here?"

"Verity. Cherish's cousin."

Morticia dipped the long white feather into the mixture, spun it once, and left it to float on the surface. The air crackled, making my fur stand on end. There was a rush of warm, cinnamon-scented air, and a second later, an angel tumbled onto the floor.

She didn't move.

I stared at Verity, then looked at Morticia. "Did the spell kill her?"

"I hope not. That would be a big waste of my time and magic." Morticia nudged Verity with the toe of her black boot.

Verity groaned and rolled onto her back. "What... what happened? Where am I?"

I walked over and hopped onto her stomach so she could see me. "Greetings! I'm Juno. And you're in Badger's Haze."

Verity's eyes flickered open. They were duller and darker than the usual brilliant blue sparkle most angels had. "How... how did I get here?"

"I summoned you." Morticia sank into a chair and gestured for me to get on with it.

"I'm confused." Verity rubbed her eyes. "I'm supposed to be working. I've just signed in for my shift, so I need to get back."

"This is work, of sorts. I've reopened the cold case to learn what happened to Cherish. You were related, correct?" I jumped off Verity's stomach as she slowly eased herself upright and looked around the dim room.

"I'm really back in Badger's Haze?" she murmured.

"You are. I hope you don't mind the summons," I said. "Time isn't on my side, and I want to get to the bottom of what happened to Cherish. You must want that, too."

Verity rubbed her forehead and took a few deep breaths. "I don't feel so good. I really need to leave."

"The spell's effects will wear off soon," I said, glancing at Morticia. She simply shrugged.

Verity looked over at Morticia. "Oh, it's you! I remember you."

"I'm unforgettable." Morticia flashed up an eyebrow.

Verity held her stomach. "What did you use to bring me here?"

"Some people call it a drag-me-to-hell spell," Morticia said.

My eyes widened. She hadn't mentioned that would be the spell she'd use to summon Verity. That kind of magic was only used in dire situations because it so easily went wrong.

Verity groaned and tipped her head back. "No wonder I feel like death warmed up."

"Is it just the spell making you feel bad?" I asked. As I examined Verity, I noticed it wasn't just her eyes that were dull. Her feathers had no shine, and several were grubby. And if she'd been about to start work, her uniform was creased, and her boots scuffed.

"If you'd felt that spell, you'd know what I mean." Verity stood slowly, one hand still pressed to her stomach.

"We won't keep you long," I said. "But I'd like to know about the time you spent with Cherish."

"Why are you investigating what happened to her now?" Verity asked. "It was such a long time ago."

"Yet her death remains unsolved," I said. "And as family, I thought you'd want to help."

Verity drew in a long breath. "Of course I do. But there was an investigation. Angel Force did everything they could. Nothing came of it."

"You're not curious?" I asked.

Verity's gaze flitted around the room. "I was. But how are you able to make any difference to the outcome of an investigation after such a long time?"

"Clues get overlooked," I said. "I've already spoken to a number of the suspects and witnesses interviewed at the time."

"We all know who it was," Verity said quietly. "But we didn't have enough proof to do anything about it."

"You're going to say Maelor?" I asked.

"Who else would it be?" Verity's expression tightened.

"Take a seat. Morticia will get you something to drink," I said, hoping a little comfort might make the angel open up.

"I don't have anything suitable for angels." Morticia slid a bottle of alcohol out of sight.

"I'm fine. I don't need anything." Verity settled into a seat and shook her head a few times, as if clearing cobwebs.

"Tell me about your relationship with Cherish," I said.

Verity sighed. "I'm not getting out of here until I answer your questions, am I?"

"I can't force you to stay," I said.

"I can," Morticia said. "While that feather is in my cauldron, you're going nowhere."

Verity's gaze flicked to the cauldron, but she made no move to grab the feather. Probably sensible.

"When I was younger, I wanted to be just like Cherish," she said. "She was so vibrant and full of life. I even joined Angel Force to follow in her footsteps."

"You wanted to work with troubled magic users, too?" I asked.

"Not exactly that," Verity said. "But our family had a reputation. Everyone held prominent positions in Angel Force, so it made sense that I'd do the same thing."

"Yet you decided to work shadow Cherish?" I asked.

"I didn't know everything she did or how closely she worked with demons," Verity said. "If I had, I wouldn't have done it. Don't get me wrong, I knew working at Angel Force came with some danger, but nothing like she faced. It put her at risk, and not just from demons. Not everyone was happy with her. They thought it was unnecessarily risky, and the results weren't worth it."

"Did you think that?"

"I was young and didn't have opinions back then," Verity said. "But speaking to other family members, I got a sense that some were worried Cherish caused more harm than good."

"To the work of Angel Force, or to your family's reputation?" I asked.

Verity ran a hand over her dull feathers. "I should go. I've got a promotion at work almost in the bag, and I can't just vanish at the start of my shift."

"As soon as you answer the questions, you're free to leave," I said.

"You make it sound like I'm a prisoner," Verity snapped. "I am sorry about what happened to Cherish, but we all saw it coming. She took too many risks and didn't follow the rules. You need to be careful when working with demons. Preferably, you avoid them or lock them up. But she always sought the good in everyone."

"You don't think demons have any goodness in them?" I glanced at Morticia, who was content to stir the cauldron and sip her drink.

"They're demons, so what do you think?" Verity shook her head. "I was so excited to train with Cherish, but after being here only a few days, I realized this wasn't the career I wanted."

"You wanted safe and mundane," Morticia muttered. "How typical of an angel not to color outside the lines of tedium."

"I'm the one who's still alive, aren't I?" Verity said. "Sorry, that sounded cold. I liked Cherish, but I was scared for her. I suggested several times that she try something different. Her work kept her away from the family for months, but we still heard the rumors about what she got up to. I wanted to see for myself."

"You were shocked when you learned the truth?" I asked.

"You know how gossip goes. Everything gets twisted until you're not sure what the truth even is." Verity licked her thumb and rubbed it across the front of her scuffed boot.

I nodded. "Do you ever visit Cherish's final resting place?"

Verity shuddered. "I was happy to leave Badger's Haze as soon as I could. It always felt so unwelcoming. But Cherish loved anything quirky and different. She was always exploring some strange possibility or going on adventures alone."

"Including the oddness in Badger's Haze?" I asked.

"I think so," Verity said. "I asked her why the village had a strange feel to it, and she said it was to do with the cemetery."

I looked at Morticia, and she nodded.

"I warned her off, but Cherish was stubborn. When she set her sights on something, she never stopped. Too stubborn for her own good," Verity said. "And that's what got her killed. She worked with the wrong demon."

"You don't seem all that sad," I said.

"I was," Verity said. "But it was an awfully long time ago. Life moves on. It gives you no choice. I wish Angel Force had found enough evidence to convict Maelor, but they failed."

"And you didn't want to pursue it yourself?" I asked. "After all, Cherish was family, and she had been looking after you, teaching you how things worked."

"I just wanted to leave and put the whole sad business behind me," Verity said.

"You didn't stay for her funeral?"

"I left, but a few of us returned. That was the last time I came here," Verity said.

"Do you remember where you were the night she died?" I asked.

"We were staying in the same house. It was housing provided by Angel Force for remote field staff. Cherish set it up, and she let me use a spare room."

"You were there the whole evening?"

"Yes. I'd fallen asleep when I got word from the housing manager about what had happened to Cherish."

"And that's the same manager who gave you your alibi?" I asked.

"Why all the questions about where I was?" Verity said. "I had nothing to do with what happened to Cherish. She was family, and I respected her. I didn't agree with her work, but I had no reason to want her dead."

"That's what you said in your original statement," I said.

"And I stand by it," Verity replied. "If you have access to all the information from that investigation, you'll see that Angel Force had no reason to consider me a suspect. They questioned me because I'd worked closely with Cherish and wanted to know if there was anyone who might wish her harm."

"And of course, you pointed at Maelor," I said.

"Everyone did! And so they should," Verity said. "I hope he got what was coming to him and led a miserable life."

"That's very un-angel of you." Morticia smirked.

"Maelor lost his way," I said. "He ended up in prison, but he's out on probation."

"I hope he's unhappy," Verity said. "That's not nice of me to say, but he was a deceitful little creep. He pulled the wool over Cherish's eyes. She thought he was a reformed character, but I'd see him skulking around, coveting things that weren't

135

his, listening in on conversations. He was always looking for trouble."

"Do you think he found it in Cherish?" I asked.

"He must have done," Verity said. "She discovered the truth about him and confronted him. Maelor struck out, and she died."

"Do you know if Cherish had any trouble with her wings?" I asked. "I'm puzzled why she didn't fly after being pushed from the bell tower."

"As far as I know, she was fine. Perhaps she was shocked and didn't react quickly enough. I guess we'll never know." Verity looked at Morticia. "I really do need to leave. If I had any useful information, I'd tell you."

"Are you done with her?" Morticia asked me.

"I think so," I said. I wasn't getting anything new out of Verity. This angel thought the same as everyone else. There was a demon in the mix, so he was the obvious criminal. So much for innocent until proven guilty.

Morticia plucked the feather from the brew, and it shriveled into a black husk. She waved her hand in the air, and Verity vanished.

"What did you think of her?" Morticia asked.

"For an angel, she looked uncharacteristically disheveled and grumpy."

"The spell I used can be a lot," Morticia said.

"It was more than that," I said. "Could Cherish's work have been too much of an embarrassment for the family? They were considered demon sympathizers because that's what Cherish was."

"Other angels wouldn't have looked on that kindly." Morticia brushed feather ash off her fingers.

"I never paid Verity much attention when she was here. She struck me as a sniveling brat, always eager to please, wandering around in wide-eyed astonishment at all of Cherish's work."

"She could have grown cynical," I said. "Panicked that Cherish's work might affect her career."

"Maybe the family sent her to spy on Cherish and report back."

"That's possible. She stays on the suspect list for now. Have you got another feather?" I asked. "We may as well question the next angel."

"I may be an incredibly powerful guardian of the dead who is feared by all, but even my magic has its limits." Morticia gestured to the door. "The spell will need to recharge. Shove off and come back tomorrow."

Not wanting to be on the receiving end of that incredible, fearsome power, I did as I was told, and high-tailed it out of there.

Chapter 15

I headed up the library stairs, dodging ghosts, and hurried to the snow globe. Tansy was curled around it, her tail flicking lazily. Sage was peering down at her with a hint of suspicion on her face.

"Hey! You made it out in one piece," she said when she spotted me.

"Morticia was surprisingly obliging," I said. "She brought the angel here using a drag-me-to-hell spell, and we spoke. Verity wasn't happy."

I updated them on my thoughts about Verity and her involvement in what happened to Cherish.

"While you were gone, I did some digging into her family," Sage said. "I asked Finn about them and got him to speak to his contacts."

"Did he find out anything useful?" I asked.

"He sure did," Sage said. "The family is a joke. And it's all because of Cherish's work."

"Even after all this time?" I hopped onto the desk and joined Tansy, my ears pricked.

"A few hundred years ago, they had an excellent reputation," Sage said. "They were invited to all the top angel events, hobnobbed with the higher angels, and got their pick of the prime postings in whatever department they wanted."

"But then things changed because Cherish opened the door to demons," I said.

Sage nodded. "Take Verity, for example. She's in the lowest role in Angel Force, and she barely scraped through the academy. She was rejected for a dozen positions before getting the one she's in now."

"That's not what she told me," I said. "Verity was keen to get back because she said she's up for a promotion and couldn't disappear."

"I can't see her ever getting out of the role she's in," Sage said. "Finn found out she's always being passed over. I think Angel Force only gave her the job she's in to keep an eye on her and ensure she doesn't drift into Cherish's line of work."

"Demon stink sticks," Tansy said. "Verity was training under Cherish when it all went wrong. The angels won't forget that."

"It's fortunate for Cythera that the demon stink didn't stick to her, too," I said.

"It's only the family who were close to Cherish at the time she died that got the reputation for loving demons," Sage said. "Cythera is more of a distant relative, so she got away with it."

"How lucky for Cythera," I murmured. "Verity looked downtrodden. Angels normally have that glittering, sparkly glow about them, but her eyes were dull, her uniform was grubby, and she gave off the air of someone who has given up."

"If Verity is being held back because of what happened to Cherish, maybe that's exactly how she feels," Sage said. "Stuck in the same dull job with no chance of anything new. That would rot the happiest of souls."

"Or Verity's feeling guilty," I said. "This information gives her an excellent motive for wanting Cherish dead. What if she realized the damage Cherish was doing to the entire family? When she started training under her, she thought she was doing everyone a favor by killing Cherish."

"When all it did was make things worse," Sage said. "The family already had a dubious reputation because of Cherish's work, and then there's a murder because of her demon meddling."

"But was it a murder Verity caused?" I asked. "She doesn't have much of an alibi. She could have snuck out of her room and gone to the bell tower."

"A motive and a shaky alibi," Sage said. "Will you question her again?"

"Not for now. Morticia sent Verity home," I said. "And I don't think I'd get anything else useful out of her. At least not until I have evidence to hold over her head."

"So, on to the next angel?" Sage asked.

"Not tonight. Morticia needs to brew more spell," I said. "But while we wait, we'll look at the next suspect's interview."

"Who's next?" Sage asked.

I rifled through the file, Tansy peering over my shoulder.

"Let's go with angel suspect number two," I said. "Lumiel. She's a relic guardian."

"That translates to geeky antiques weirdo who likes dusty old stuff no one really understands," Sage said.

I chuckled as I activated the transmission buttons to send the statement to her. "Let me know what you think."

ANGEL FORCE INTERVIEW TRANSCRIPT

Case file: #32-1875

Conducted by: Angel Gideon
Interviewee: Angel Lumiel

GIDEON: Thank you for agreeing to speak with me. I understand this is a trying time.
LUMIEL: Cherish's death was a terrible thing. She was diligent, courageous, and undeserving of such an end. I only wish I could have done more to prevent it. I knew of her work with demons, so worried about her safety, but this is too sad. It should never have happened.
GIDEON: You're currently serving as guardian of celestial relics?
LUMIEL: I am. I maintain the ledgers and records of angelic artifacts recovered from demonic activity or other unlawful possession. Cherish consulted me when an investigation

crossed into my jurisdiction.

GIDEON: You worked closely on many cases?

LUMIEL: Indeed. Cherish was one of the few who understood the delicate nature of relic work. Many see it as dull or administrative, but she understood the need to catalog and store powerful items.

GIDEON: Did you notice anything unusual in her behavior leading up to her death? Any signs of distress or fear?

LUMIEL: None that she shared with me. But she spoke often of her frustration with how Angel Force restricted her work.

GIDEON: What restrictions bothered her?

LUMIEL: The need for daily reports and having an angel assigned to each demon to monitor their behavior. She said it wasn't needed.

GIDEON: Did Cherish have concerns about working with any particular demons?

LUMIEL: There was one demon she often talked about. Maelor. You have caught him, haven't you? He was her latest project, allegedly informing on other demons. But demons are masters of deception, so I didn't trust him.

GIDEON: Did you have much to do with Maelor while you were in Badger's

Haze?

LUMIEL: I don't work with demons, but I was here because he'd handed over fragments of an angelic halo. It was a remarkable find. Well, I say he found them. He must have stolen them.

GIDEON: How did Maelor behave around such rare items?

LUMIEL: He seemed drawn to them, covetous, even. I made a note of it and warned Cherish that such fascination could not lead anywhere good.

GIDEON: Did Cherish take your warning seriously?

LUMIEL: No. She saw goodness where others saw danger. That was her greatest strength, and, it seems, her undoing.

GIDEON: You suspect Maelor killed her, then?

LUMIEL: I do. He wouldn't have been able to resist wanting to use the relics. They carry immense power. For a demon to touch them, well, I believe he was poisoned with longing. He wanted what no fallen creature should ever have.

GIDEON: Do you have proof of this?

LUMIEL: Cherish confided in me that she was meeting someone the night she died, but she didn't say who. I'm convinced it was Maelor.

GIDEON: Where were you that

evening?

LUMIEL: In my quarters, reviewing relic reports. I have a room in the same complex as Verity and Cherish.

GIDEON: Did anyone see you there?

LUMIEL: My hours are solitary. I need silence when working. I went to bed and was woken with the tragic news.

GIDEON: And after you learned of Cherish's death?

LUMIEL: I checked every record connected to Maelor and then contacted my superior and told them the demon had to be involved. Cherish died because she trusted too deeply in something irredeemable. She deserved better than to be struck down by a creature she was helping. I hope you catch him.

GIDEON: Thank you. Your statement will be added to the official record.

LUMIEL: I only hope it helps you find the truth. If I can help in any other way, please let me know. I'm at your disposal.

FOLLOW UP

Lumiel provided full cooperation. Her testimony reinforces the theory of demonic involvement. There are no grounds for further inquiry into her conduct.

Chapter 16

"If that's not leading the witness, I don't know what is." Tansy had her wrinkled nose pressed close to the aged paper.

"Angel Force focused the same token amount of interest on Lumiel as they have the other suspects," Sage said.

"Other than Maelor." I nodded. "The angels couldn't believe one of their own would do this."

"Which is short-sighted," Sage said. "But not surprising."

"Lumiel sounded helpful and sad about what happened to Cherish," I said. "Maybe she'll still feel the same way and want to talk to us."

"I can get Finn to help with finding her," Sage said. "If Lumiel is still active in the service, he'll be able to contact her."

"Do it discreetly," I said. "We don't need Cythera getting wind that we're poking at all the angels."

"You're the one dealing with her at the moment. Just keep her busy and she'll be none the wiser." Sage looked over her shoulder. "Vorana's back. I'll find out how her spa sleuthing went and then get on to Finn." She disconnected the snow globe.

I wandered the library and was pondering what to eat when stomping footsteps approached. I recognized that familiar stomp, so barely looked around as the sound cut off at the end of the bookstack.

"It's no good ignoring me," Cythera said.

"I'm not," I said. "I'm just clutching at a few more seconds of peace before you tell me off."

She let out a sigh. "We need to talk."

I turned and looked at her. "About what, exactly? I know you think I'm a thorn in your side, but I want to help figure out what happened to Cherish. That's the real reason you're here, isn't it?"

"I know what you're doing," Cythera said. "I get regularly hassled by Sage, Vorana, Zandra, and anyone else who thinks you should be back in Crimson Cove."

"That must keep your days busy," I said.

"More than I want them to be," Cythera said.

"But you've been listening to the updates from Sage, haven't you?" I asked. "You know about the two cold cases I've solved."

"You're not solving them because you have a heart of gold," Cythera said. "You're solving them because you think it'll get you off your sentence."

I wrinkled my booping snooter. There was an ulterior motive behind what I was doing, but righting wrongs was always top of my priority list.

"Perhaps at first that was my focus," I said. "But there's something so satisfying about solving these cold cases."

"You mean especially when Angel Force failed to do so?" Cythera glared at me.

"That's an added bonus." I stepped closer. "I know I haven't always followed an honest path, but I've been better since coming to Crimson Cove with Zandra. Sometimes I've acted in my own self-interest, but I always make sure the criminals get what they deserve. And that's what I'm doing here."

"So you can get back to Crimson Cove," Cythera said.

"Don't you want to find out what happened to Cherish?"

"I already know what happened."

"Then tell me!" I said. "Because all I've discovered is prejudiced fingers pointing at a demon suspect, but no evidence strong enough to determine if he's the killer."

Cythera stared at me, and I stared back.

"I'll go first, shall I? Cherish worked with demons, which wasn't a popular choice," I said. "But for the moment, I'm less interested in that. What else did she work on?"

"What do you mean?" Cythera asked.

"She had her demon informers, but she uncovered something else while she was here. Do you know what that was?"

Cythera's nostrils expanded. "That's none of your business."

"I'm already figuring it out. You can help or stay out of my way, but I'll solve this," I said.

Cythera sighed and leaned against a bookshelf. "Cherish was the black sheep of the family. Always breaking the rules, much like you."

"Sometimes you need a rule breaker to shake things up and make change," I said.

"Change is a hassle," Cythera said. "Cherish was an embarrassment to the family. Yes, she got results, but by working with troubled individuals who caused chaos and sent the rumor mill into a whirling frenzy."

"Just because she didn't stick to the rules doesn't make her a problem," I said. "Cherish broke the mold. Being different should be supported, not squashed."

Cythera stood up straight, her wings flaring. "Breaking the mold is what got her killed!"

"Then help me get Cherish justice," I said. "I know she was on to something big in Badger's Haze. She was figuring out what was going wrong with the village, wasn't she? Is that what got her in trouble?"

Cythera tipped back her head and stared at the ceiling. "I don't know. We barely spoke back then. Most of the family didn't speak to her."

"That must have been tough on her," I said.

"I guess, but back then, I listened to what everyone else said."

"Which was?"

"Don't get involved with Cherish, so I didn't."

"But you're older and a little wiser now," I said. "Why don't we finish what Cherish started?"

"Because I don't have a death wish," Cythera said.

"Fine. I do," I replied. "And I still have two more angels to speak to about what happened to Cherish. You can make that happen. Be part of something good."

Cythera glowered at me. "Leave this alone, or you'll end up just like her." She turned and stomped away.

I let out a breath, watching as a trail of white feathers drifted through the air currents. I wasn't leaving this mystery alone. I was solving it, even if it meant getting trapped here forever. I'd make sure Cherish's killer was caught.

⁂

"We have an innocent suspect! Nix didn't do it," Sage said through a mouthful of bacon. "Vorana's spa research yielded results. Plus, she no longer has a backache thanks to the amazing massage she got."

I pushed a few pieces of dried kibble around on the desk. "That's good."

"You don't seem happy that Nix is innocent," Sage said.

"I am. And I'm glad Vorana had a nice day at the spa."

"It's kind of amazing," Sage said. "There were still some of the original staff there. The place is run by hope goblins, and you know how long they live. They even had a few old photographs of Nix with the staff. She was an amazing tipper, which is why she was so fondly remembered."

"That's good. I'm glad we can cross someone off the list." I pushed away the kibble. I'd been awake all night, thinking about how to resolve my issues with Cythera. She was digging her heels in so hard over this investigation.

"And I have more good news," Sage said.

"You're bringing me home?" I asked.

"Not quite that good. But I've connected with Lumiel. I can bring her into our conversation now."

I looked up. "That was fast! Finn found her easy to get hold of?"

"She's semi-retired from Angel Force but still works for them a couple of days a week," Sage said. "Finn tracked her down, told her what you were doing, and she said she was happy to help."

"What are we waiting for? Let's see what we can find out."

"Give me a second to get the connection stable."

The snow globe hissed and buzzed before Sage vanished. Then she reappeared, a smaller version of herself in one corner of the globe. In a separate image appeared a mature, radiant angel with a swirl of blonde curls.

Sage made the introductions.

"It's a pleasure to meet you," Lumiel said. Her voice had a rich, honeyed undertone. "I was surprised when I received a message explaining what you were doing, but I'm happy to assist. Even though it happened such a long time ago, it never sat right with me that Cherish's death remained unsolved."

"How closely did you work with Cherish?" I asked.

"We didn't work together daily, but our paths would often cross," Lumiel said.

"You worked with the informers, too?" I asked.

"Not directly," Lumiel said, "but they would often bring their objects to Cherish, and she would ask me to review them. I'm a relic guardian. I record objects of value or relevance in our archive. It's the largest record of celestial objects in existence, dating back many thousands of years. Quite an extraordinary place to visit."

"What would you do with an object or relic when it was discovered?" I asked.

"I make a written record, create images, and then test its ability," Lumiel said. "All under controlled conditions. Some objects still contain extensive power, so they need proper handling and storage. Others have grown unstable after decades of neglect, so they need to be contained to ensure no one is harmed."

"What about object misuse?" I asked. "If someone used a celestial relic for misdeeds, for example, would you know about it?"

Her mouth turned down at the corners. "Sadly, that happens. We receive objects that have been tainted with something foul. They are cleansed and kept in isolation for a minimum of six months before being retested to see if the magic has stabilized. If it has, it's moved into the main archive."

"That must be a hugely powerful collection of objects," I said.

"Indeed, it is," Lumiel said. "And they're closely guarded, as is the exact location. Some people don't always use magic for good, do they?"

"That's where I come in," I said. "Can you remember the demon Cherish was working with when she died?"

"After your friend contacted me, I double-checked my ledgers," Lumiel said. "The demon you speak of, Maelor, brought pieces of halo to Cherish. It was part of their deal."

"From my understanding of angel halos, they're extremely rare," I said.

"Rare and immensely powerful," Lumiel replied. "I couldn't believe it when Cherish contacted me and said this demon possessed such objects. I told her to take them off him. He handed them over willingly, apparently."

"You don't sound convinced by that," I said.

"A lower-class demon like Maelor could change his entire existence with such power," Lumiel said.

"Perhaps he thought offering the fragments of halo to Cherish would show he was sincere."

Lumiel's expression tightened. "I don't have such a generous heart when demons are in the mix. I didn't trust Maelor, and when I visited to take possession of the fragments, I could clearly see how much he coveted them."

"Do you think he wanted to use them but didn't have the power to do so?" I asked.

"Quite possibly," Lumiel said. "Cherish thought highly of him, though, and told me he'd already provided valuable information which would lead to the arrest of several demons."

"But that wasn't enough for you to think his intentions were good?"

"Angels are raised to believe demons are our natural enemy, and I struggled to unite that upbringing with the evidence of Maelor's reformed character."

"You were in Badger's Haze on the night Cherish died, weren't you?" I asked.

"That's right, but I didn't see Cherish in the evening," Lumiel said. "She went out, and I stayed up late studying relic reports."

"Is it usual for you to stay up so late working?" I asked.

Lumiel chuckled. "My career is my passion. I consider myself fortunate that I turned something I adore doing into a paid job. Few can say that. You could ask any of a dozen angels I work with, and they'd tell you I'm often burning the midnight oil."

"When did you hear about what happened to Cherish?"

"The man who managed the housing ran along the corridor and knocked on Verity's door. I heard the commotion and went to see what was going on. It was chaos after that."

"In your initial statement, you seemed convinced Maelor was involved," I said. "Are you still?"

"Very much so," Lumiel replied. "Maelor was more powerful than he admitted to being. I believe he was working to unlock even more power to manipulate the halo fragments. He realized Cherish was about to hand over the fragments to me for study, and he needed to stop her. I'm certain they argued that night, and he destroyed her."

"How do you know he was more powerful?" I asked.

"It was more of a feeling than actual evidence. But he would watch Cherish intently. He sought a way to take back what he'd given her." Lumiel sighed. "Something that powerful will often sway weak minds to do terrible things."

"Even something as pure as fragments of halo?"

"If corrupted." Lumiel was silent for a second. "I'm so glad you're looking into this case with such dedication. I often think about Cherish. If you'd like me to visit, I'd be happy to assist."

"Thank you. I may take you up on that," I said.

"I hope that demon gets what's coming to him," Lumiel said. "He's brought nothing but bad luck and harm to anyone he goes near."

"It seems that way," I replied. "I may need to speak to you again."

"I'm at your disposal, whatever you need, so long as we find out what happened to Cherish," Lumiel said.

We said our goodbyes, and I sat back, pondering everything I'd heard.

"You think it was Maelor, too, don't you?" Sage asked.

"It seems so obvious," I replied. "But why didn't Angel Force charge him with murder?"

"They were being too cautious," Sage suggested. "Maybe they didn't want to risk a feud with the demons."

"They're always feuding with demons," I said. "Whatever the reason, I need to bring Maelor in and make this official."

A gloomy sky greeted me as I headed out of the library, walking toward the shabby inn where Maelor had a room.

There was no one at the reception desk, so I made my way along the lower floor, sniffing until I caught the faint scent of sulfur drifting from under a door. I was about to knock when I noticed it was ajar.

I pushed it open and poked my head inside.

Maelor lay motionless on the floor.

Chapter 17

I raced into the room and jumped onto Maelor's chest.

His breathing was labored, his eyes fluttering, and his skin slick with sweat.

I jumped up and down several times to get him to stir. "Maelor, it's Juno. Wake up!"

Looking around the room, it was clear there'd been a struggle. The bedclothes were on the floor, as if someone had dragged Maelor out of bed while he slept. A lamp had been knocked over, its base smashed along with the bulb.

I pressed my paws against Maelor's face and attempted a healing spell. It fizzled and slammed into the wall. I shook out my paws and tried again, more tentatively this time. The spell shimmered around my toe beans but refused to take.

"Please work," I whispered to my faulty powers.

I tried again. This time, the magic shot out, circled me, and wrapped around my tail before yanking me into the air. I howled in disapproval and shook the spell off, dropping back onto Maelor's chest.

His breathing grew fainter. If I didn't do something fast, I'd lose him and any hope of determining his guilt in this murder.

I dashed out of the inn and almost collided with Cythera, who was on her way inside.

"What are you doing here?" she said.

"Someone's attacked Maelor. Help me save him!" I turned and ran, and a few seconds later the floor thudded as Cythera followed me back into the room.

"He's probably had too much to drink." Cythera peered at Maelor, a sour expression on her face.

"He's injured. Look at him!"

"So, revive him," she replied.

"If I had any real magic left, I would," I said. "But someone made sure that was ripped from me in a cruel miscarriage of justice. An injustice that burns brightly in my heart even now. An injustice that—"

"You did that to yourself."

"Heal him!" I said. "Angel energy can fix almost any injury."

Cythera pressed her hands into her armpits. "Why should I? He killed Cherish."

"You don't know that for sure," I said. "Maelor may have been the prime suspect, but Angel Force never charged him. That means there wasn't enough evidence to convict."

"Everyone knew he did it," Cythera said.

"Then don't you want to make sure he stays alive so he can serve his sentence behind bars?"

"We should leave him here." Cythera shifted from foot to foot. "It's not as if he's of any use. He's just taking up space and causing problems."

"Unless a demon has possessed you, you'll fix him," I said.

She stared down at Maelor, who was now barely breathing. "He doesn't deserve to be saved."

"He also didn't deserve to be yanked from his bed and knocked unconscious," I said. "We need to know why he was attacked."

Cythera crouched beside Maelor and placed a palm on his chest. "He was attacked because he's an untrustworthy, dangerous demon who destroyed someone I cared about."

I stepped back as a wave of her golden energy flooded over Maelor, starting at his chest and radiating out until it dripped off his fingertips. When his breathing settled and his eyes flickered, Cythera stood and stepped back, wiping her hands across her shirt.

"Thank you," I said.

"I've done the bare minimum." Cythera nudged Maelor with the toe of her boot. "Get up. I want answers from you."

"Give him a moment," I said. "It looks like he took quite a beating."

Cythera shrugged, completely unsympathetic.

"Maelor, it's Juno. Can you hear me?" I asked. "What happened here?"

Maelor groaned, his eyes slowly opening. He stared at the ceiling for a second, then turned his gaze toward me. "What are you doing here?"

"I came to ask you a few more questions about Cherish, and I found you unconscious on the floor," I said.

He exhaled slowly. "I think someone came in here. I was asleep, but suddenly I was moving, and then I got hit with something. I don't know what."

I looked around the room. There was no sign of a weapon. "It must have been magic."

"Get on your feet and stop wasting our time," Cythera said.

Maelor's head whipped toward her, and he cringed away. "Was it you?"

"Of course it wasn't me!" she snapped. "I wouldn't waste my time on a lowlife like you."

"That's enough," I said. "Maelor was working with Cherish. He was being helpful, and perhaps he still wants to be."

"I do!" Maelor said. "It's why I came back."

"Well, you came back because it's part of your new probation terms," I said, "but I appreciate the sentiment. Tell me what you remember about your attacker."

Maelor's gaze slid around the room. "Nothing. Like I said, I was sleeping when they laid into me. The first thing I was aware of was flying through the air and being dumped on the floor. Then an enormous pressure slammed into me."

"You didn't catch a glimpse of who did it?" I asked.

"They were fast and strong. That's all I can tell you."

"What about a smell?" I pressed. "Anything that could help me figure out who did this."

Maelor struggled up onto the bed and ran a hand down his face. "It doesn't matter. It's not as if you can help me."

"I can, and I want to," I said. "No one deserves to be attacked in their sleep. That must have been terrifying."

"It happened too quickly for me to be terrified," Maelor said. "Thanks for helping, though. You didn't have to. Maybe you shouldn't have. You could have just left me here."

"You would have died," I said.

"It's not as if I have much to live for," Maelor muttered.

"Put a hold on the pity party," Cythera said.

Maelor winced again and cringed away from her. "I don't want any trouble. I came here because I heard Cherish's case was being looked into. Have you got any news?" he asked me.

"I've spoken to all but one of the other suspects from the initial investigation," I said.

Maelor sighed. "Let me guess. They've all pointed at me. I didn't do it. I promise. But no one believed me back then, and you won't believe me now."

"I believe in truth and evidence," I said.

"Do you have enough evidence to convict me?" Maelor asked. "Because if you do, it's not real."

"Actually, no," I said after a second of hesitation.

"But we'll find it." Cythera grabbed hold of Maelor's T-shirt and yanked him to his feet. "Why did you do it? Why did you murder Cherish?"

"I didn't! I liked her. She was one of the few people who wanted to spend time with me." Maelor hung limp in her hold, making no effort to fight back.

"You were there on the night she fell from the bell tower." Cythera shook him. "Cherish shouldn't have trusted you, but she always thought she knew better."

"Be careful," I said. "Maelor's still recovering."

"He doesn't deserve to recover. He deserves to rot in a cell," Cythera said. "Confess what you did that night!"

"I didn't do it." Maelor grabbed hold of Cythera's hands, but he didn't try to hurt her. "Cherish looked out for me when no one else did."

"She was only interested in you because of your knowledge," Cythera said. "She didn't care about you or want to help you."

"She did! Cherish was good like that. She always had time for me," Maelor said.

"You're delusional and a liar." Cythera lifted him off his feet.

I jumped onto Cythera's shoulder and dug in my claws. "Unless you want to go away for murder, calm down and let Maelor go."

Cythera flared her wings to knock me off, but I held on tight.

"I know you're hurting and angry that Cherish is dead, but this solves nothing," I said. "We need to find evidence to get a conviction. Shaking the truth out of Maelor won't work, and even if you get a confession under these circumstances, it won't hold up in a trial."

Cythera hissed out a breath, then dropped Maelor and stepped back. "I shouldn't have saved him."

"But you did because, even though you hide it well, you have a good heart," I said.

"I have a naïve heart. A heart that shouldn't listen to you." Cythera lifted me and dropped me onto the bed.

Maelor was also back on the bed, shaking from head to toe. I rested a paw on his arm to help calm him.

"I need to know everything about what Cherish was working on just before she died," I said. "I understand she discovered something big. Something that impacted Badger's Haze."

"How do you know that?" Maelor asked after tearing his fearful gaze from Cythera.

"Because I'm extremely good at my job, even though I don't get paid for it." I flicked a glance at Cythera. "Ever since I was sent to Badger's Haze, I've known something is wrong with this place. Was that what Cherish was working on?"

Maelor took a few seconds to settle himself. "When I first reached out to Cherish, I wasn't sure what to expect."

"You should have expected a long sentence in prison," Cythera said.

I shushed her and gestured for Maelor to go on. He took his time before continuing.

"I was in trouble with some higher-level demons," Maelor said. "They promised they would ruin my life before destroying me. I had to find a way out before it was too late."

"That was when you contacted Cherish and told her you had fragments of an angel halo?" I asked.

He nodded. "We came to a deal."

"What kind of deal?" Cythera asked.

"I stole the fragments of halo from another demon," Maelor said. "Once I'd done that, it was game over for me. I'd never be able to go back home, so I had to make sure Cherish would look after me."

"And did she?" I asked.

"She was amazing," Maelor said. "I was suspicious at first, but we met several times, and she showed me her plans. There was a safe house for me, and a new identity. I could start again somewhere no one knew me."

"Was that the only deal you made with Cherish?" Cythera asked.

"There was a bit more to it than only getting a fresh start," Maelor said. "I knew what the halo fragments could do, and I also knew what the demon I stole them from planned to do with them. It wouldn't have ended well."

"That must have been a powerful demon if he could corrupt such angelic objects," I said.

"Yeah, he was the worst," Maelor said. "Anyway, once I'd met Cherish and we'd agreed to work together, I asked for something else."

"I knew it!" Cythera said. "Demons are tricksters."

"No! It wasn't a trick. Cherish needed my demon energy to reveal the corruption forced on the halo fragments," Maelor said. "In return, I asked if she'd give me a power boost."

"You manipulated Cherish into giving you access to angelic power," Cythera said sharply. "I suppose you were going to use it for good, weren't you?"

"I don't really know what goodness is," Maelor said. "I might have used it to have some fun, but nothing bad. All I wanted was a quiet life and not to have to watch my back when I was out in the world alone. Cherish wouldn't protect me forever. I had to make it worth my while."

"Was she foolish enough to give you some of the halo's energy?" Cythera's expression was full of disbelief.

"It almost happened," Maelor said. "But then she died. So, you see, I'd never have murdered Cherish because I needed her. She was the only way I could boost my power and have a fighting chance. With her gone, I was back to the same old, same old."

"Why did you disappear so quickly after she died?" I asked.

"Running makes you look guilty," Cythera said.

"After Angel Force finished questioning me, I knew what was coming, so I disappeared. I've been living off the grid, talking to no one, seeing no one, just existing. Honestly, it's been miserable."

"It's no less than you deserve," Cythera said. "You manipulated Cherish for your own gain."

"Because Maelor was desperate," I said. "We've all had moments like that."

"You may have," Cythera said coldly.

"Can you really not remember anything about the person Cherish was meeting on the night she died?" I asked Maelor. "You were there, and you had a view of the bell tower."

"I've gone over it so many times in my head," Maelor said. "But there's nothing I can pull from my memories that reveals who she was with."

"Because it was you!" Cythera said. "Just confess. You've already revealed you have nothing in the way of a life. This is your one path to redemption. Admit the heinous crime you committed, and then you can rest easy."

"There'll be no rest for me if I go to prison," Maelor said. "The demon I stole the halo fragments from had connections everywhere, including inside any prison you send me to. Some of his friends are still alive. I'd be lucky to last a week."

Cythera shrugged again as if that cold truth didn't bother her.

"Did Cherish ever confide in you about the troubles in Badger's Haze?" I asked.

"She was worried about energy signatures," Maelor said. "She thought she might be able to unlock the halo power and do a deep cleanse. That's how she described it."

I looked up at Cythera. "Would that have worked?"

"It might have when the initial malaise took over," Cythera said. "But this is basically an abandoned village. The only people who stay here are those who can't leave. And there's something about this place that drags people back."

"I've heard that mentioned before," I said. "But there must be a way to reverse the damage. Cherish was on to something."

"She was in over her head, and look what happened to her," Cythera said. "We have her killer in front of us."

Maelor jumped up. "I should leave. I'm only causing problems by being here. I wanted to help, but I've made things worse."

"You're going nowhere," Cythera said. "You need to answer for this crime."

Maelor dodged around her, but Cythera grabbed his shoulders.

"Let me go! I'm innocent," Maelor said.

"Stop fighting me," Cythera said. "You're making yourself look even more guilty, if that's possible."

Maelor shouted as Cythera held on. She attempted to fold her wings around him, but he pressed a hand against her feathers, and the sharp smell of burning filled the air.

"You both need to calm down," I said. "We'll find a solution that doesn't involve murdering each other."

"The only solution is for this monster to go to prison," Cythera said.

They tussled for a few more seconds, and I was about to intervene when the door opened. An angel I vaguely recognized stood there. She took in the scene, raised her hands, and blasted Maelor with a dazzling surge of golden energy.

He groaned, released his hold on Cythera, and collapsed.

Chapter 18

I checked Maelor was still breathing, then stomped toward the new arrival. "Why did you do that?"

"Cythera was in trouble. She needed saving," the angel said.

"She had control of the situation, and we were just getting to the bottom of a mystery. Who are you anyway?" My fur stood on end as I glared at the angel.

"We spoke through the snow globe."

I tilted my head and studied the angel more closely. "You're Lumiel?"

This angel bore a vague resemblance to the one I'd spoken to, but she looked much older and had shorter, spiky blonde hair.

Lumiel blushed. "I use filters. I'm an embarrassment to my family for not aging with grace."

"Those are some effective filters," I said. "But I understand the pressure of having to look the part. When it comes to physical appearance, societal demands are unpleasantly troubling."

"It's a pleasure to meet you in person." Lumiel smiled, a little shyly. "Your reputation precedes you."

I was about to preen and puff out my chest when I realized she'd spoken to Cythera!

Cythera had been studying Maelor, but she looked up sharply at that comment. "You know who I am?"

"Of course. I've seen your picture on the award boards at the Academy. Everyone speaks highly of you. I hope I didn't overstep by assisting. That demon appeared to be causing you trouble."

Cythera's mouth pressed into a thin line. "Maelor wasn't a threat, but he wasn't behaving as he should. These demons are all the same."

Lumiel stepped further into the room. "Oh! I didn't recognize him. He's also aged badly. He's shrunk!"

"Maelor isn't a problem," I said. "And he had important information we needed, and now you've knocked him out."

"Is that all my magic did?" Lumiel peered down at Maelor. "He must be much more powerful than he used to be if he could withstand that blast."

"You intended to kill him?" I stared in disbelief at this angel. Maybe it wasn't just her appearance that embarrassed her family.

"When another angel's life is under threat, you must act." Lumiel looked down at me. "You seem surprised I'm here. I told you I was coming."

"You didn't," I said. "You offered your help, but we made no agreement that you would come to

Badger's Haze. The place has never seen so many angels."

"I'm sure I mentioned it. I want to help you figure out what happened to Cherish," Lumiel said. "It was such a shock to hear that name spoken again. Although I often think about her, she did such wonderful work with the most undeserving of characters."

"You mean Cherish gave troubled magic users a second chance," I said.

"When it came to the characters she assisted, it was more like the tenth or eleventh chance," Lumiel said.

"It can take people a while to find the right path," I said.

"Some never find it," Lumiel replied. "This demon, for example, only ever showed signs of ill intent."

"Did you see him ever act on that intent?" I asked.

"Naturally. He's a demon. When I visited Badger's Haze to record information on the halo fragments, I could tell he was up to no good."

"He may have been back then, but he's doing no one harm now," I said. "Let's get him somewhere safe and give him time to heal."

"Why don't I take him in?" Lumiel suggested. "Everyone knew he was guilty back then. Maelor is a foul, loose end that was never snipped off."

"He hasn't confessed! And there's not enough evidence for a conviction," I said. "Besides, you've injured him, although you weren't the first. When I got here, I found him barely breathing."

"I'll take him into custody, get him treated, and then we'll talk to him," Lumiel said. "Maybe after all these years, he wants to repent."

I didn't want Maelor out of my sight until I'd gotten all the information from him. I nudged him a few times, but he didn't stir. I looked up at Cythera for support, but from the stubborn set of her jaw, she had no intention of offering him more healing energy.

"We'll take Maelor to the library," I said. "He can sleep it off under my watch."

"You can't trust a demon!" Lumiel said.

"This one may be untrustworthy, but he's going nowhere," I said. "You can come back with me if you like, to keep an eye on things."

Lumiel turned to Cythera. "Is this acceptable?"

"It's not ideal, but nothing about this case is."

"Then it's agreed. Maelor stays with me," I said. "I'll need someone to carry him."

"I suppose I'll have to do that," Cythera huffed, then bent and lifted the demon into her not-insubstantial arms.

We headed out of the inn and walked back to the library in tense silence. When we reached the steps, Lumiel stopped and looked around.

"I don't like the feel of this place. The last time I was here, the energy felt wrong, too," she said. "It's not gotten any better."

"That's what I was talking to Maelor about," I said. "He knows something about Cherish's work. She was looking into the strange energy and figuring out what had gone wrong."

"Probably too many demons visiting," Lumiel said.

I snorted softly. Here was an angel unafraid to display her demon bias.

"Let's get inside." Cythera stomped up the steps and kicked open the door she hadn't broken, leading the way upstairs.

I hurried ahead to make sure there was no sign of Sage in the snow globe, but it was empty.

"What do you want me to do with Maelor?" Cythera asked.

"Set him down on the couch in the corner," I said. "Mice have chewed it, but it's comfortable."

Cythera placed him on the couch and stood looking down at him. I joined her as Lumiel took a moment to explore the library.

"You know I'm right about Maelor," I murmured. "I think the attack happened because he had information on Badger's Haze and why it feels so wrong."

"Or they attacked him because he killed Cherish and they wanted revenge," Cythera said.

"That would put you on the suspect list."

Cythera grunted a response to my comment. "It could have been a local who liked Cherish. They recognized Maelor and got their revenge."

"I've spent enough time in this village to know that's unlikely," I said. "Residents look after their own needs first and don't bother with anyone else. It makes no sense that anyone local would commit an act of revenge after so many years have passed."

"You don't know everyone here," Cythera said. "And that's deliberate. Before you arrived, I warned them to stay away from you because you're unstable."

"How charitable of you," I said. "It's taken me a long time to get anyone to so much as speak to me."

"I'm glad they listened to my advice," Cythera said.

I let out a breath. "You don't think it's strange that someone tried to kill Maelor? I was about to speak to him because I was almost convinced he killed Cherish, but this attack throws everything into question."

"It doesn't," Cythera said. "He's guilty."

"Maelor was never popular," Lumiel said as she walked over to join us. "I like Cythera's idea that it was a vengeful resident teaching him a lesson."

I still wasn't convinced by that theory, but while Maelor was out cold, he was of no value to me, and we needed forward motion.

"While we wait for Maelor to recover, I have one more statement to review," I said.

"You haven't been through them all?" Cythera asked.

"I've skimmed them, but I take each one and pull it apart to make sure Angel Force didn't miss anything."

"We never miss things!" Cythera looked away, having the good grace to be embarrassed by that blatant lie.

"Whose statement do you have left to look at?" Lumiel asked.

"Aurek," I said. "He was part of the team sent to monitor Maelor while he worked with Cherish."

"Don't waste your time with him," Lumiel said. "He won't have anything to do with this."

"I'm speaking to everyone Angel Force interviewed after Cherish died," I said.

"His statement is only on file because he was around at the time of the murder," Lumiel said. "He's a friend. I trust him with my life."

"Even so, I must speak with him," I said. "And since you're close, ask him to visit Badger's Haze. Tell him why he needs to come here and stress the urgency."

"Don't go giving orders to an angel. Behave," Cythera snapped at me.

"You behave by doing your job properly," I said. "Aurek could have useful information. You'd do the same thing if you were sifting through a cold case and reviewing the suspects."

"Stay here and try not to cause trouble." Cythera caught hold of Lumiel's arm and moved her out of my hearing range. They bent their heads close together, debating what to do next.

While they talked, I snuck to the snow globe and gently patted it.

"I'm here," Sage whispered. "What's going on?"

"The angels are going round in circles, as usual," I whispered back. "While they figure things out, we've got one more statement to look at. I'm sending it through now."

ANGEL FORCE INTERVIEW TRANSCRIPT

Case file: #32-1875

Conducted by: Angel Gideon
Interviewee: Angel Aurek

GIDEON: Please state your full name and position in Angel Force for the record.
AUREK: Aurek. Lead Envoy. My role involves overseeing demon cooperation projects.
GIDEON: You were sent to Badger's Haze for that purpose?
AUREK: Yes. I arrived three days before Cherish's death. My task was to monitor Maelor's activities and report back to Angel Force regarding his usefulness and compliance.
GIDEON: How well did you know Cherish?
AUREK: We worked together during her visits to various outposts. She was one of our most capable officers, deeply committed to reforming demons.
GIDEON: When did you last see her alive?
AUREK: The evening she died. I encountered her near the bell tower.
GIDEON: And how did she seem?
AUREK: Distracted, troubled. I asked

if she needed assistance, but she said she was meeting someone and would be fine.

GIDEON: Did she mention who she was meeting?

AUREK: No, but I assumed it was Maelor. He'd been restless earlier that day, pacing near the boundary line. It looked like he was thinking of leaving.

GIDEON: You spoke with him?

AUREK: No, observation only. I don't engage with the demons I monitor unless essential. It's an anthropological art. I ensure compliance and construct a catalog of demon behavior and attributes. It always helps to know thine enemy.

GIDEON: You saw him that night?

AUREK: I glimpsed him near the bell tower shortly after speaking to Cherish. He looked agitated, but he disappeared before I could get any nearer to see what concerned him. I believe he went inside to find Cherish.

GIDEON: Did you follow him?

AUREK: I started to, but I had an urgent summons from a villager. There was a child who had taken ill, so I left to heal her. By the time I returned, the alarm had been raised, and Cherish had already fallen.

GIDEON: What time did you leave the bell tower to assist this sick child?

AUREK: It must have been just before midnight.

GIDEON: Did anyone see you at the sick child's home?

AUREK: The child's mother, Mrs. Halloway. She can confirm I arrived and stayed until just after one in the morning. I used a basic restoration charm. It was nothing elaborate, but it broke the mild hex someone had placed on the child.

GIDEON: You mentioned Cherish seemed troubled. Did she tell you why?

AUREK: She'd been worried about something connected to the cemetery. She said she'd uncovered traces of corrupted energy and was close to solving something, but others were standing in her way.

GIDEON: Did she say who?

AUREK: She didn't name them. But we need no stretch of the imagination to figure out who was behind this malevolence. The stench of demon is everywhere.

GIDEON: Do you believe Maelor killed Cherish?

AUREK: Who else? And he was near the bell tower that night.

GIDEON: Why would he kill her?

AUREK: Does a demon need a reason to act with malice? I suggested more caution, but Cherish was fearless.

GIDEON: Is there anything else you wish to add?
AUREK: Only that Cherish deserved better. She was brave and will be a great loss to our work.

FOLLOW UP

Confirm Mrs. Halloway's testimony regarding Aurek's movement (although he is not considered a suspect.)
Re-examine demon Maelor's whereabouts during the same window and question him regarding his presence at the crime scene.
Review Cherish's correspondence regarding any corrupted energy near the old cemetery.

Chapter 19

The scent of burned coffee beans drifted up from the library's lower floor. Cythera and Lumiel had marched off to discuss next steps, which, judging by the clatter of cups and low muttering, translated to drinking overly strong coffee and finding new ways to exclude me from the conversation.

I nudged the snow globe. The glass shimmered, and Sage's face came into view.

"I've just finished reviewing Aurek's statement," she said.

"It's another angel pointing at the demon." I sighed. "Doesn't it seem too convenient? Like they've put their heads together to ensure Maelor looks guilty."

"Or maybe he looks guilty because he is guilty," Sage said.

I nodded slowly. "Maybe. That's where I was headed until the attack."

"What about the follow-up actions from Angel Force?" Sage asked. "Did anything useful come out of that?"

I shuffled through the case file. "Mrs. Halloway confirmed Aurek visited because one of her children was sick, but she couldn't say exactly when."

"Which means his alibi is as solid as soggy toast," Sage said.

"Angel Force also checked Cherish's papers about corrupted energy, but nothing came of it. They must have looked about as hard as a mouse looks for salad."

Sage chuckled. "So, nothing useful. Keep pushing. Something will crack."

"I just hope that something's not me." I glanced toward the door as muffled voices drifted up.

Footsteps thumped up the stairs, and a moment later, Cythera returned without Lumiel.

"Where's your new best friend?" I asked.

"She's gone to look around Badger's Haze. Not that it's any of your business," Cythera said. "You were disrespectful toward her. She didn't deserve that."

"Lumiel wants to convict Maelor before he's even pleaded his case," I said. "That's hardly the action of a sensible, level-headed angel. Besides, she's not even part of Angel Force, so she can't take people in and interrogate them."

"Her division is closely associated with our work," Cythera said. "That gives her the right to make an arrest in the face of adversity."

"That was hardly an adverse situation," I said. "You had Maelor at your mercy. Lumiel could see that. She didn't have to knock him unconscious."

"She was doing what she thought was best," Cythera said. "As we all are."

"However, you've finally seen sense and realized this mystery isn't so straightforward?" I asked.

"I always see sense!" Cythera folded her arms. "But I agree that we need to be thorough. This is an old case, so something could have been overlooked. I've already summoned Aurek, and he's on his way. He won't be long."

My mouth dropped open. "Spending time with me is doing you good. You're developing new ways of thinking."

"And developing new ways of getting rid of you for good," Cythera said.

"You've already done that," I replied. "Or have you forgotten how cruelly you banished me here?"

"I know exactly what happened." Cythera slumped into a seat, her wings sagging.

"Admit it," I said. "You're missing me, aren't you? I made your life easier when I solved the difficult crimes in Crimson Cove and let you write up all those fascinating reports."

"You made my life extremely complicated," Cythera said. "But sometimes your input was valuable. Not your sassy attitude, though. Definitely don't miss that."

"You miss every single piece of me," I said. "Even the white fur glitter I left on your desk."

"That was highly annoying." Cythera glanced up at me, then heaved out a labored breath. "I think I'm burned out."

I was so surprised by her confiding in me that I couldn't speak for a few seconds. "Is it because of your marriage problems?"

"My marriage is a disaster. My home is a mess. And work is a nightmare because I'm not there." She waved her hand at me. "I just can't find a reason to bother with anything anymore."

I rested a tentative paw on her knee. "That's not you talking. The same thing happened to me when I first arrived in Badger's Haze."

"What do you mean?"

"It's this place," I said. "It messes with you. I was a depressed, miserable muddle who barely ate and spent all day napping. Fight it. It's the only way to keep going."

"But what am I fighting for?" Cythera asked. "I'm always defeated by something. I'm failing at life."

"That sounds tough. And your problems are only compounded by not having me as your ever-trusty support and expert guide."

She growled at me. "It's never felt this difficult."

"Tell me about the problems back home," I said. "I've had a few hints, but I know there are issues in Crimson Cove."

"Yes! Issues I should be dealing with, not messing around with you, trying to solve an ancient case that outwitted the best angels."

"They were only outwitted because they didn't have me."

Cythera slid me a glare from the corner of her eye. "The angels who look after the laws are the very best in the business. They all go through the academy. They know what they're doing."

"But things were different back then," I said. "I'm interested in the fragments of halo. They're not in the evidence box. Do you know where they are?"

"They should have been sent to containment," Cythera said. "Check with Lumiel. She deals with celestial relics."

"If I could examine them, I might get some clarity."

"You're not getting your paws on them," Cythera said. "You'll use them to get back to Crimson Cove."

My ears pricked. "They really have that much power?"

"Don't push your luck," Cythera said.

"Can we come to an agreement?" I asked. "This case must mean a lot to you. I know you said you were here to assess my progress, but Cherish was a relative. Even if she was the black sheep of the family, you must want to know what happened to her. Get some resolution."

Cythera let out a slow breath through pursed lips. "Of course I do. No one talks about Cherish anymore, but there's still the unsolved murder hanging over the family. What agreement do you have in mind?"

"If I help you solve Cherish's murder, will you let me go back home?"

"That's outside my control," Cythera said. "The higher angels passed your sentence."

"Then will you talk to them so they see sense?" I asked.

"They don't listen to me. They never listen! They're always showing up, wanting meetings and talking about new ways of working." She sighed again. "Sometimes I think they just visit for their own amusement."

"You're admitting the higher angels are quirky?" I asked.

"They're a pain in my behind," Cythera said. "They've been a constant source of irritation since you left. Your problems have affected me."

"I never cause problems. I only make solutions," I said. "And one solution to focus on is figuring out what happened to Cherish."

There was a thump on the main library door.

"That must be Aurek," Cythera said. "Let's get this over with."

"I'm glad we have the spirit of cooperation working again," I said.

"It's the spirit of someone who's exhausted and has nowhere else to turn," she muttered. "I'll go let Aurek in so you can question him. But no sass. Keep things professional."

Cythera left and returned a moment later with a striking-looking angel who had the usual dazzling blond hair and piercing blue eyes. She made the introductions before leaving to grab coffee for both of them.

"There's no need to be nervous." I noticed Aurek glancing around and rubbing his hands together.

"It's hard not to be. I pick up emotional resonance," he said, his voice low-pitched, smooth, and oddly soothing like an angelic version of Barry White.

"And what emotional resonance have you picked up since arriving?" I asked.

"Spiky tension, anxiety, depression." He inched closer. "I felt that coming off Cythera, too. I hope it doesn't affect me."

"So long as you don't linger, you'll be fine," I said.

Cythera returned with two mugs of coffee and nothing for me. We all settled into hardback chairs at a table.

"As I'm sure Cythera told you," I said, "I've reopened the investigation into what happened to Cherish. You were in Badger's Haze when she died, weren't you?"

Aurek nodded, scratching absently at the back of his hand. "It happened such a long time ago, but I remember it."

"How well did you know Cherish?" I asked.

"We worked together on and off for years," Aurek said. "She was great at her job. She'd sometimes skirt close to the line to get results, but it always worked."

"I get the impression not everyone was happy with her work with demons," I said. "What did you think about that?"

"It was odd. But I was glad she had such an open heart and mind to work with demons and get them to help us. I don't think I could ever do that." He leaned forward. "I heard Maelor was here. Is that true?"

"He's in this very building," I said. "Someone attempted to kill him."

Aurek jerked back. "What happened to him?"

"We don't know for certain there was an attack," Cythera said. "It's possible his injuries were self-inflicted."

"It's very un-possible they were self-inflicted," I said.

"Heavens above," Aurek murmured. "I was surprised to learn Maelor was alive. He didn't have fans in the demon community, and after killing Cherish, the angels hated him, too."

"You're certain Maelor murdered Cherish?" I asked.

"It has to be him." Aurek set his mug down with a shaky hand. "I even saw Maelor that night. He was skulking around the bell tower."

"He admits he was there on the night Cherish died," I said. "He saw her fall."

"I watched him for a few minutes, and then he disappeared," Aurek said. "He must have gone into the bell tower."

"What were you doing at the bell tower?" I asked.

"My job," Aurek said. "Monitoring Maelor. I would follow him to see what he was doing. I'd also sit in on his interviews when Cherish spoke with him."

"Was the information he gave her useful?" I asked.

"Most of the time, yes," Aurek said. "It seemed legitimate that he wanted to help bring in troublemaking demons."

"But you still didn't trust him."

"He was a demon! What else is there to say?" Aurek glanced at Cythera.

"Remind me again of your movements after you saw Maelor at the bell tower," I asked.

"It's all in my original statement," Aurek said. "I was planning to go into the bell tower, but a villager's child needed help. I followed her to her house and healed the child."

"In the statement, the lady you assisted with the poorly child wasn't exact on her timings."

"I don't blame the poor woman for that," Aurek said. "She was stressed from having an unwell child. But I was there, I assure you. And I had great respect for Cherish. I'd never want anything bad to happen to her. I just wish I'd gone into that bell tower. I could have stopped this from happening."

Cythera stood. "Thanks for the visit. Sorry we wasted your time."

I wasn't done with the questioning, but a glare from Cythera kept my mouth shut.

"If there's anything more I can do to help, just let me know," Aurek said as he stood, leaving his untouched coffee. "I hope you find enough evidence to convict Maelor. It's never sat right with me that he got away with it."

"I'll show you out," Cythera said.

I darted a look at the snow globe. Sage was watching.

"What did you think of that?" I asked the second they'd left the room.

"Aurek seemed okay," Sage said. "Nervous though, don't you think?"

"I get that there's a weird vibe in Badger's Haze," I said, "but is that enough to unsettle an angel? I'm going to follow him, see what he does next."

"Make sure Cythera doesn't catch you trailing an angel. I can hear those stamping footsteps from here. She's not happy with you."

I hurried away and hid in a book stack until Cythera gave up looking for me and stomped off, then dashed down the stairs and out of the library. In the distance, Aurek was striding away.

I raced along after him, jumping over puddles and muddy slush. Rather than heading to the edge of the village and flying off, he turned toward the old cemetery. When he arrived, it took him a few minutes, but he got through the protection wards and entered.

Since I had a safe rite of passage thanks to Morticia, I continued after him. It felt good not to get warning pings and stings of magic to tell me I was misbehaving, and I slid effortlessly past the gate.

Aurek headed to Cherish's grave. He rested a hand on the top of the headstone and hunched over it.

I crept closer, just enough to hear what he was muttering.

His breath came out in shaky bursts as he swiped a hand across his nose. "I will never forget you. I'm sorry I haven't been to visit in such a long time, but you know what it's like."

I edged closer. That wasn't the tone of someone visiting an old colleague. Aurek sounded broken.

"Don't think my love has faded," he continued. "I will always be here for you. And I'm here for you now, to make sure Maelor gets what's coming to him. The demon will pay for taking your precious life."

I crouched behind a headstone, my heart pounding. Aurek had been in love with Cherish.

But had she loved him back?

Chapter 20

My paw knocked a stone loose, and Aurek's head shot up.

I ducked and held my breath, certain I hadn't been seen, although with this white fur, you could never be perfectly concealed.

"Who's there?" Aurek called out.

I had two options. Slink away or confront a murder suspect who'd been keeping secrets about his relationship with Cherish. I had approximately three of my nine lives left, and I was feeling lucky, so I stepped out from behind the headstone.

"Greetings! I didn't mean to spy on your moment of mourning, but I am curious about what I overheard."

Aurek scrubbed at his eyes with the heel of his palm. "Go away! You had no right to do that. This is my business. Stay out of it."

"You forgot to mention in your original statement to Angel Force, and to me, when I just questioned you, that you were excessively fond of Cherish."

"Because that had nothing to do with what happened to her," Aurek said.

"It's often a motive," I said.

"What are you talking about? Didn't you hear me? Go away."

"Unrequited love," I said. "There's often a thin line between love and hate. You clearly adored Cherish, but if she didn't return your feelings, things could have soured."

"That's... that's not what happened."

I walked closer. "Were you in a romantic relationship with Cherish?"

"What does it matter now?" Aurek snapped. "It was a long time ago."

"It may have been a long time, but I see from your reaction to visiting her grave that you still have feelings for Cherish."

"I'm leaving, and don't follow me or I'll report you to Cythera," Aurek said. "She told me about you."

"I'm sure Cythera painted a vivid picture of how incredible I've been in solving the cases Angel Force failed to," I said. "And to be clear, I always figure out whodunit."

"If you think you can solve anything by looking at me, then you're making a big mistake." Aurek's wings flared as he turned and marched away.

I hurried to keep up with his long strides. "If you talk about it, you'll feel better."

"I'm telling you nothing. Why bother? Maelor is the killer."

"So everyone keeps saying." I had to break into a jog to keep up with him. "Why didn't you reveal your relationship with Cherish during the interview?"

Aurek broke into a run, looking like he was preparing to take off. Before he launched into the air, a fizzling bundle of black fury and fur leaped out from behind a mausoleum and latched onto a wing.

Aurek yelped, lost his balance, and slammed into a crumbling headstone, pitching face-first into the dirt. Midnight hung off Aurek's wing, his claws scoring deep into the feathers.

"That was impressive." I slowed to a trot and caught up with them.

"Morticia told me to keep an eye on things," Midnight said through a mouthful of feathers. "Make sure you didn't get yourself into too much trouble." He chewed on a long white feather, looking far too pleased with himself for bringing an angel to heel.

"The assistance is welcome," I said. "Although I could have taken him."

"The dude was about to fly. Unless you were about to grow wings, you'd have lost him," Midnight said. "Is this our killer?"

"Get off me!" Aurek sputtered. "Who are you?"

"I can't do that until you promise not to fly away," Midnight said. "And you're in my cemetery, so you follow my rules. If I say you stay, you stay."

"That's right." I stamped my paw into the dirt for dramatic effect. "Running only makes you look guilty."

"You already have Cherish's killer. Why waste time looking at me?" Aurek asked.

Midnight snorted a laugh. "You were making a run for it. You may as well have stamped *guilty* in indelible ink on your forehead."

"Let me up," Aurek said. "I promise I won't fly away. I was upset. That's all."

Midnight glanced at me, and I nodded. He dropped to the ground but stayed close, his hackles lifted.

Aurek stood and brushed dirt off his once immaculate clothing. "May I go now?"

"Not yet," I said. "Talk to me about Cherish. You had feelings for her, and they haven't faded. Were you together?"

Aurek inhaled and exhaled slowly several times before leaning against a giant slate-gray mausoleum, his shoulders rounded and his head down.

"Start talking, or I shred those feathers," Midnight said.

"I adored Cherish," Aurek said quietly. "She was different from any angel I'd ever met. She cared nothing about what other people thought of her and had a passion for making sure justice was done."

"Cherish sounds like a fine angel," I said. "And I share her sentiments. That's why I reopened her case. She never had resolution. That's unfair."

Aurek sniffed back tears. "I still don't understand why Maelor wasn't charged with her murder."

"There wasn't enough evidence," I said. "And being a demon doesn't automatically make you the worst magic user in the room. I wish it did, but that's not the case. You often find the most innocent face hiding the darkest secret."

"What secrets are you hiding?" Midnight perched himself on a nearby headstone and was washing his face with a paw, although his steely gaze remained on Aurek.

"Nothing!" Aurek slid him a glare. "I kept my feelings about Cherish to myself because I didn't want to complicate things."

"You lied in your interview," I said.

"Because it's not relevant to what happened," Aurek said.

"Does that mean she had feelings for you, too?" I asked.

Aurek chewed on the side of his nail, staring ahead but not really looking at anything. "I thought she might. She was always kind and happy to listen to me. But when I suggested we go on a date, Cherish said she didn't have the time. She was focused on her work, which was her one true passion."

"It was a case of right angel, wrong time?" I asked.

Aurek barked a misery-tinged laugh. "Cherish said something similar. I told her I was happy to wait, but she said it wasn't fair on me."

"She gave you the brush-off," Midnight said. "She wasn't into you."

I gently shushed Midnight. "How did you feel about that rejection?"

"Hurt, of course," Aurek said. "But I didn't want to give up hope. I thought I could win her round. I started with gifts, and when I realized she cared nothing about material things, I went hunting for something she'd adore."

"Chocolate," Midnight said. "Chicks love chocolate."

"Not chocolate," Aurek said, though a faint smile flickered across his face. "Although she had a sweet tooth. Cherish loved frosted brownies with crumbled pecans mixed in. I used to bring her a box every time I visited."

"If her only passion was righting wrongs," I said, "does that mean you brought her cases to investigate?"

"I brought her leads," Aurek said. "Information about demons who might be turned, so they'd inform on others."

"That sounds risky. You must have visited some shady places to get those contacts."

"I had more than a few feathers burned over the years," Aurek said. "But Cherish was always grateful when I supplied the names."

"But her feelings never grew beyond gratitude?" I asked.

"She seemed to forget about me after I introduced her to Maelor." Aurek scowled at the ground.

"You knew Maelor before Cherish did?"

Aurek nodded. "I never met him before he came here, but I heard whispers that he had information about some higher-up demons causing us trouble. I put out feelers, found out where he lived, and passed it to Cherish. What a mistake. That got her killed. I got her killed."

"You couldn't have known what would happen," I said. "Cherish knew the risks."

"But if I hadn't introduced her to Maelor, he wouldn't have killed her!"

"Maybe he didn't," Midnight said. "It could have been you."

"It wasn't me," Aurek growled.

"You have an excellent motive," I said.

"I adored Cherish. Even though she didn't want me like that, I was still willing to help her. I just wanted to see her happy."

"You don't have the most reliable alibi," I said.

"And as I told you, it was a long time ago, and memories fade," Aurek said. "I went to help that sick child, so I couldn't have been with Cherish when she fell. And if I'd seen it happen, I would have caught her. She'd still be alive."

"A dodgy alibi and rejected by the angel you loved. I say you're guilty," Midnight said.

Aurek's expression darkened, but he didn't respond. His grief looked genuine, and sorrow wove through his words. He seemed broken as he spoke of Cherish.

"Are you only saying Maelor is the killer because of what he is?" I asked. "We all know demons have a terrible reputation, but when I spoke to Maelor, he didn't seem that devious."

"Cherish spent most of her time with him," Aurek said.

"And that made you jealous?" I asked.

"Yes, but not in the way you're thinking," Aurek said. "Maelor was useful. He'd been a general runaround for higher-up demons for a long time. They usually forgot he was in the room, so they shared information that no one else should know. He tucked that away and became a fountain of useful knowledge that we made use of."

"But you still think little of him," I said.

"He turned on his own kind," Aurek said. "Why would anyone trust him?"

"Cherish did," I said.

"This sounds like an age-old story of jealousy to me," Midnight said. "If I were you, Juno, I'd lock this one up and throw away the key."

"You'd be locking up the wrong person," Aurek said. "I'm here to help. I want Maelor put away for what he did."

"It won't happen unless he confesses," I said. "There wasn't enough evidence to convict Maelor the first time around. That's why he walked away."

"You mean he got away with murdering the most wonderful angel ever to walk this earth?" Aurek's voice cracked, and he sniffed back more tears. "I don't know what to do. Coming back here, I thought I could be useful, but it's too painful. I should leave."

"Stay and help," I said. "You'll find resolution when we discover who really killed Cherish. It won't be easy, and you'll feel sad, but that's natural. Let those tears drop. Feel the pain. It's all part of the healing process."

Aurek swallowed several times. "I want to help. And... there's something I haven't been completely honest about."

"I knew it!" Midnight said. "Here's your killer. The shiny-faced angel pretending to be sad."

"I am sad! And I don't have a shiny face. I use oil blotting sheets." Aurek ran a hand down his face.

"What haven't you been honest about?" I glared at Midnight, willing him to take a break from riling Aurek in case he stopped confiding in me.

"The night Cherish died, I was at the bell tower," Aurek said. "And I was called away by a worried villager who had a sick child. But... the person I saw going into the tower that night wasn't Maelor. I'm still convinced he did it, though."

"You lied in your statement about seeing Maelor!" I said. "That lie could have got him charged with a murder he didn't commit."

"I know he did it! I'm certain of that, so I had no problem saying he was there," Aurek said.

"You're as delusional as you are blond," Midnight said. "You've got some poor, innocent demon up to his neck in trouble because you made assumptions."

"Demons are never good news," Aurek spat. "He took all of Cherish's attention and time, especially after he showed her those halo fragments. I remember the day she told me what he'd brought her. I'd never seen her eyes shine so brightly, or her smile so big."

"Celestial relics of that power are hugely valuable," I said. "Especially since Maelor stole them from demons who would have used them to do untold amounts of damage."

"Yes, I know, and I was happy about that," Aurek said. "But after Cherish had the halo fragments, I barely saw her."

"And we're back to the jealousy motive," Midnight said.

I didn't disagree. This looked bad for Aurek.

"I knew that night Maelor would be lurking about somewhere close to Cherish," Aurek said. "It wasn't a lie just because I didn't see him."

"It was so a lie," Midnight said.

"Let's put that to one side for a moment," I said. "You were at the bell tower. If you didn't see Maelor, who did you see?"

Aurek hesitated before his top lip curled. "That covetous jerk who was always creeping around Cherish after she got her hands on the halo fragments."

"There are so many covetous jerks in Badger's Haze," Midnight said. "You'll need to be clearer."

"Yahir Hallow," Aurek said. "He saw Cherish go into the bell tower, and he followed her."

Chapter 21

"We need to drag Yahir out of the ground and speak to him again," I said. "Find out what he was doing inside the bell tower when he told Angel Force something different."

"That won't work." Midnight shook his head. "You shouldn't drag ashes out of the ground more than once. They won't re-mold properly. I'll be chasing bits of Yahir around the village for weeks. And I'm not doing that."

"I have to! I need to find out what he was up to that night."

"Search what's left of his house," Midnight said. "There could be something useful there."

"The place is still standing after so much time has passed?" I'd already turned toward the corner of the cemetery where Yahir rested.

"It stayed in the family. They tried to sell it a few times, but with the fire damage and issues with the foundations, no one wants it," Midnight said. "There was talk of turning it into a community hub with a museum attached, but then Badger's Haze went to the dogs, and everyone lost interest. No one is buying property here, and no one visits, so the already messed-up house was left to rot."

With some reluctance, I led the way out of the cemetery, Aurek and Midnight following me.

"Even though I saw Yahir that night, he's not the killer," Aurek said. "It was Maelor."

"You're letting your prejudice show again," Midnight muttered.

"What was Yahir like around the halo fragments?" I asked.

"Well... he was obsessed with relics," Aurek said.

"And when he learned Maelor had brought the fragments into Badger's Haze?"

"He was beside himself with excitement. It was all he talked about. He even asked me once if I could convince Cherish to loan the fragments to him so he could explore their potential."

"You didn't mention that." I slowed when I noticed Midnight wasn't following us out of the cemetery. "Is something wrong?"

"I should stay," Midnight said. "Something is stirring underground. This place isn't used to having so much company, so things are interested in coming out."

I nodded in understanding. "Thanks for your help."

"Anytime I can be bothered, I'll have your back."

"Where do we find Yahir's house?" I asked.

"Head straight. Third right. Take the next left. Look for the sagging thatched roof and blue door with the wonky walls. It stands alone on a plot. You can't miss it." Midnight turned and slunk into the cemetery, magic already sparking on his paws.

"Did Yahir ever examine the power in the fragments?" I asked Aurek as we continued to Yahir's home.

"Maybe. I know Cherish was angry with him once," Aurek said. "She wouldn't give me the details, but she said he'd gone too far and should keep his hands to himself."

"Was he inappropriate with her?"

"It wasn't that! Maybe Yahir tried to take the halo fragments without permission and got caught by Cherish." Aurek shook his head. "None of this matters."

"It does if Cherish stopped Yahir from stealing the fragments."

"They had a good relationship," Aurek said.

"Until he went too far and tried to take what didn't belong to him," I said. "If Yahir had tried that, would he have been able to control the angelic energy?"

"He had power," Aurek said. "Monitoring and cataloging old, unstable magical objects requires great skill."

"Yahir was lurking around that night, hoping to convince Cherish to let him borrow the halo fragments," I mused. "Or maybe he decided he'd take them, anyway. Did Cherish carry the fragments with her?"

"Sometimes. She'd gotten worried that too many people were interested in them," Aurek said. "She often kept them on her."

"Maybe Yahir arranged to meet Cherish at the bell tower," I said. "Would she have thought that unusual?"

"Cherish often met people in odd places at unusual times," Aurek said. "She had no choice, since she dealt with dangerous characters or people who were wanted by Angel Force. She needed to be discreet. And she could look after herself, so I doubt she'd have feared meeting Yahir. After all, he wasn't at all intimidating."

"He was intimidating enough if he shoved Cherish out of the bell tower, and she was powerless to stop it," I said. "And you said he had skills."

"I still don't trust that demon," Aurek said. "Focus on him."

"The only crime Maelor is guilty of is being a demon. His life's been ruined because of people's prejudice."

Aurek had the good sense to look ashamed. "It's what we're taught at the academy."

"Those teachings need to be updated," I said.

"The war between angels and demons has been raging forever, and I never see it ending."

"I understand your inbuilt bias. History like that leaves a mark. We'll discuss how important it is to change minds once we've solved this case." I stopped outside Yahir's home, which was just as Midnight had described, and peered through a window. "I don't see anyone in there."

"Are we breaking in?" Aurek took a step back.

"Since this is an emergency, we have no choice." I tested my magic and found it willing, so I applied it to the door lock and pushed the door open.

A quick look around told me there was no one home, and there'd been no one home for a long time. The place had an eerie silence, the contents of each room a thick layer of dust, and from the scrabbling noises in the attic, hosted at least one party of rats.

I spent a few minutes in a large room surrounded by smoke-damaged, crumbling wall hangings showing hundreds of grave rubbings. It looked as if Yahir had rubbings from every headstone in Badger's Haze. There were also framed pamphlets advertising local shows he'd attended to showcase his rubbings.

We headed up the stairs. There were only two bedrooms. One was clearly a guest room, but the other had a large double bed and a closet full of moldy clothing.

I crouched and peered under the bed. A glint of something caught my eye, and I wriggled further in to get a closer look. I drew in a sharp breath. It was a fragment of angel halo.

A shiver ran through me as its power radiated out and tickled my paws. I caught hold of it carefully and wriggled back until I was out from under the bed.

"Aurek! I found something. Take a look."

Aurek appeared in the doorway and gasped. "Juno, do you know what that is?"

"I can take a good guess from the energy it's giving off," I said. "Why has Yahir got a halo fragment stashed here?"

"Has he had it all this time?" Aurek sounded awed, his eyes wide as he peered at the tiny, sharp-edged slice of halo.

"Maybe he took it from containment," I said. "What do you think he was planning to do with it?"

Yahir hadn't seemed like a threat or even a serious suspect when I'd spoken to him. This made no sense. Why was this fragment here? Had it been lurking under this bed all this time, and never been discovered? That seemed unlikely.

There was a crash downstairs as the front door slammed open, and a few seconds later, footsteps thundered up the stairs. Lumiel burst in, holding a small glowing gadget.

"It's here, isn't it?" she said, her tone high-pitched.

"Um... Greetings! What are you looking for?" I asked.

"I monitor activity around ancient angel relics. I got a ping a moment ago, and it led me here." Her gaze cut to the halo fragment, and she sucked in a breath.

"This must be what your gadget alerted you about," I said. "We just discovered it under Yahir's bed."

Lumiel's mouth dropped open. "You know what this means?"

"We were just figuring that out," I said. "Your input is welcome."

"It's obvious! Maelor planted it here. He wants us to think such a respectable historian would misuse an ancient relic," Lumiel said.

"That's impossible. Maelor is out cold in the library after you blasted him off his feet," I said.

"Then he did it earlier. That scheming demon!" Lumiel inched closer to the relic, waving her device around. "There's still power in the fragment."

"I doubt it was Maelor. After I interviewed him, he went to the inn. He most likely holed up, awaiting his fate," I said. "Then you attacked him."

Lumiel frowned. "Are you sure he didn't sneak in here and plant that piece of halo? When was the last time you saw him?"

I hesitated. Maelor might have recovered and left the library, but how did he get his hands on the halo fragment?

"We should check," Aurek said. "To be on the safe side."

"If Maelor got hold of the fragment, wouldn't he use the power against us?" I asked.

"Maybe he planned on doing that after framing Yahir." Aurek held out a hand. "I should take the fragment."

"I'm the expert on relic objects," Lumiel objected. "It should stay with me."

"Neither of you is touching this," I said. "I'll look after it. And if either of you takes it from me, I'll consider you guilty."

"Of what?" Lumiel asked.

"Murdering Cherish to get the halo fragments."

They shared a look.

"Keep it somewhere safe," Aurek grumbled. "If any demons learn this fragment is in circulation, they'll come for it, and be happy to turn you into a pair of mittens if you get in their way."

"It'll be safe at the library." I balanced the fragment on my back between my shoulder blades.

"Let's move. There's a demon to apprehend." Lumiel turned and dashed away, Aurek following.

I hurried after the angels as they dashed down the stairs and out the door.

"Maelor wants to cause maximum chaos," Lumiel said. "He's done this to distract us."

Her argument didn't convince me, but there'd be no use debating until she saw Maelor was in the library, recovering on the mouse-chewed couch.

We raced to the library, hurried inside, and I spotted Cythera heading into the main room with a mug of coffee in her hand. She slowed when she heard us thundering toward her and turned around.

"Is something wrong?" she asked.

"Where's Maelor?" I said.

Her gaze flicked to my back. "Is that—"

"Yes, a piece of rare and powerful angel halo. Where's Maelor?"

"Probably in the same place he's been since you dumped him on the couch," Cythera said.

"Are you certain?" Lumiel dashed past with Aurek.

"Not completely, but he was there the last time I looked," Cythera said. "I've just come up from the archives, so I haven't seen him for a while."

"He's not here!" Lumiel yelled. "I knew this had the foul stench of demon about it."

I ran over, and sure enough, Maelor was gone. I turned toward the snow globe. Sage would have been watching his movements, so she'd know what happened.

My stomach dropped. The globe lay on its side on the floor. I was about to dash over and see if it still worked when I realized Cythera was watching. If I let on that the snow globe was how I accessed Crimson Cove, she'd take it away.

"Never trust a demon," Lumiel growled out. "He's behind all of this mess. He has been from the start. Maelor acts pathetic and weak, but he has a devious mind. He tricked Cherish, and now he's attempting the same with us. I won't stand for it."

"You almost killed him!" I said. "That was no trick. And Maelor was struggling to recover from your angelic blast of righteousness. I can't see how he got back on his feet so quickly, somehow located and then stole the halo fragment, and had time to plant it under Yahir's bed."

"Maelor could do pretty much what he liked if he accessed that fragment's power," Aurek said. "Slow time, transport himself from one location to another with barely a blink of the eye. With that power in his hands, he could make a mess of this entire investigation."

I turned to Cythera. "You didn't hear or see anything strange when you were in the archives?"

She shook her head. "The last time I looked at Maelor, he was unconscious. His breathing seemed even, but I didn't see him as any threat."

"Then you're as naïve as Cherish was," Lumiel said.

Cythera glowered at her. "You let Maelor spend too much time with Cherish. You should have reported that he was a danger to her and had the relationship terminated."

"Everyone Cherish worked with was dangerous," Lumiel said. "She was cautioned to be careful, but you know what she was like."

Cythera rubbed her forehead with the tips of her fingers. "Cherish was never reckless, though. Not until Maelor revealed the halo fragments. I remember her talking so excitedly about them."

"So do I," Lumiel said with a sigh, some of the anger fading. "I should have been more insistent that I take them and double-check whether the magic was contaminated. But Cherish was so sure it felt pure and wouldn't harm anyone."

"Unless the fragments fell into the wrong hands. Word got out about their existence," Aurek muttered, "and then every creep crawled out of the woodwork wanting to get their slimy little hands on them."

"We need to hunt down Maelor and stop him from doing more damage," Lumiel said.

"What damage?" I asked. "Maelor doesn't have the halo fragment. I have it."

"There are more!" Lumiel turned away. "We must find Maelor. He's trying to frame innocent people because the net is closing in on him."

I looked back at the couch. Had I ignored the obvious for too long? Everyone said Maelor was behind this murder. But he'd seemed genuinely remorseful that he'd lost the opportunity Cherish offered. A boost of power would have changed everything for him. What would have caused him to lose that chance by killing his protector?

"I'm all for keeping an open mind and giving people second chances like Cherish did," Aurek said, "but this demon has gone too far. We need to bring Maelor in and show him he can't mess with us."

I looked at Cythera, and she lifted one shoulder. "If Maelor is on the loose, we need to stop him and ask him some questions."

"Let's go." Lumiel gestured to Aurek and Cythera. "We'll split up and fly over the village. He won't get away with this."

"Wait!" But they were gone before I could say another word.

I growled as control slipped through my paws.

I hurried to the fallen snow globe and tapped it. It crackled a few times, but Sage's face didn't appear. She must have been caught watching. That was why the globe got damaged.

Without Sage's support, who would help me?

The air chilled, and Tansy popped into view, followed by several of the library's ghosts.

"Oh dear," Tansy said. "You've got yourself into something of a pickle, haven't you?"

"I don't know what's going on," I admitted. "Everyone thinks Maelor is behind this chaos and the murder, but I'm not convinced."

"You're right not to be," Tansy said. "I was hiding on top of a bookshelf with my new friends, and we saw everything! Maelor isn't a killer or a thief."

Chapter 22

"Tell me what you saw," I said. "Did someone take Maelor?"

Tansy drew in a breath, her eyes gleaming with excitement. "Oh, yes. And it was the most magnificent golden energy I've ever witnessed. It was so dazzling, I struggled to watch."

A library ghost spread out his arms as if about to give a Shakespearean monologue. "It was a sight my eyes devoured because of its beauty! It reminded me of—"

"I'm telling the story." Tansy poked a paw through his middle. "You weren't here for the first part, but I was, and I saw it all."

Another ghost twirled around me. "Such energy, such vibrancy! It was a tonic to my withered soul."

Tansy hissed at him. "Shush! All of you. I'm telling the story."

"We don't have time for this," I said. "Who snuck into the library and whisked Maelor away?"

"I'm trying to tell you, but these buffoons won't be quiet," Tansy said.

"We can't be silent about something so magnificent," a ghost declared. "The joyous nature of that power, filtering through this dusty old space, warmed my bones."

"You don't have bones," Tansy said. "You're a full ghost. I have bones, so I tell the story."

I groaned. "Will one of you please tell me what happened? Everyone thinks Maelor planted a halo fragment in Yahir's old house to mess with the investigation, but unless he did it while he was unconscious, it definitely wasn't him."

Tansy shooed away the ghosts and did a big stretch. "The ghostly buffoons are right. The energy that took Maelor was magnificent. And there's only one source of magic I know that looks like that."

"Which is?"

Tansy drew in another deep breath. "Angel magic."

I took a step back, though the revelation shouldn't have surprised me. There were three angel suspects in this investigation.

"What was Cythera doing while Maelor was taken?" I asked.

"She had nothing to do with this," Tansy said. "I didn't see her after she went into the basement, although I heard plenty of grumbling and un-angel-like cussing. That angel has a filthy mouth on her."

"The potty-mouthed angel could be involved," a ghost with a ruffled neck collar said. "I've floated around this place longer than most, so I've seen a thing or two. Angels can deceive, even though they hate to admit it."

"Let's focus on the angel suspects we already have," I said. The idea of Cythera being involved in this mystery made my head spin. "Did you see an angel nearby just before Maelor was taken?"

Tansy shook her head. The ghosts copied her.

"Aurek changed his story after I discovered his unrequited love for Cherish," I said. "At first, he said Maelor went into the bell tower, but then he admitted he lied and it was Yahir."

"A double deflection. Most ingenious," a ghost said. "It's got to be him."

"Who him?" I asked. "Yahir or Aurek?"

"Stop confusing Juno," Tansy said.

"There's also Lumiel," I said. "She's been helpful, but maybe too helpful so she appears innocent, when there's hidden guilt."

"What about the halo thingy left in Yahir's house?" Tansy asked. "How did that get there?"

"It was poorly hidden," I said. "And not covered in dust or cobwebs like the rest of the house, so it hadn't been there long."

"Planted?" Tansy asked.

I nodded. "Lumiel thought so. She insisted Maelor planted it."

"It was the killer," the ruffle-wearing ghost said. "Find out who planted that shiny fragment, and you've solved the case."

"Well done, Einstein," Tansy said.

"I knew him!" A fresh-faced ghost drifted in. "Terrible manners. And never brushed his hair. Clever, though."

Tansy gestured for the ghosts to get lost. "There's also Verity, isn't there?"

"Yes. An angel desperate to restore her family's name. A name soiled by Cherish's work," I said.

"Verity also lied about being up for a promotion, when the truth is she's been stuck in the same dead-end job because of the demon slur on her family name."

"Frustrated in her career, she commits the worst sin?" Tansy asked.

"There is your killer," the new ghost declared.

"Buzz off and haunt somewhere else," Tansy said. "We're figuring out something important."

"Neither Aurek, Verity, nor Lumiel have perfect alibis," I said. "So it must be one of them."

"Our killer is an angel." Tansy blew out a breath. "How do you take down an angel?"

I gulped back my panic, my gaze flicking to the snow globe. I needed Sage. She would figure out a magic boost so I could take on an angel and survive. But with the globe out of action, I had no way to contact her.

"I need five minutes," I said.

"Where are you going?" Tansy asked.

"I'll be back. Don't worry about me." I slunk along the book stacks, heading to the area where the oldest and most powerful texts were kept.

I hurriedly scanned the spines of the old, worn books, resting my paw against each one to find a flicker of magic that might attach itself to me. Nothing stirred.

I'd been complacent about practicing the old ways and could only conjure basic spells, much to Sage's disgust. How I regretted that now.

Whatever old magic I stirred up would still be nothing compared to an angel's power. Especially one I needed to take down because they were a killer.

A small spark of magic hit a toe bean, and I shuffled the book out. Flicking through the pages to find inspiration, I whispered, "There must be something here. Give me a sign I'm on the right path."

The book remained stubbornly silent.

A softly cleared throat came from behind me, and I glanced over my shoulder to see Tansy watching.

"Are you looking for a particular spell?" she asked.

"Something that will make me strong enough to defeat an angel," I said. "No big deal."

"You're in the right section. Let's look together. It'll take less time." Tansy floated over and joined me. "Sorry about the ghosts. They're jealous of how alive I look compared to them."

"They're fine. I'm used to them." I turned more pages. "I'll miss them when I'm gone."

"You're definitely planning on going home?" Tansy asked as she shuffled out another spell book.

"This was only ever temporary. And now Cythera is here, I'll get her to see sense," I said.

"That must be nice, to have a home to go to." Tansy had her nose pressed close to a page, but I didn't miss the flicker of sadness in her eyes.

"You don't consider Badger's Haze home?" I asked.

"Not really. Mind you, I've spent so much time here, I suppose I should consider it home. But you know that feeling you get when you're in a place and it settles on you like your favorite warm blanket?

You imagine yourself digging in roots and becoming part of the community. That's not here for me."

"Do you have a place that's ever felt like that?"

"It was so long ago I barely remember," Tansy said.

"Maybe you'll become one of those nomad types, you know, always drifting around, especially since you now literally drift."

"That could be fun for a while," she said. "But exhausting if you do it for too long. If you don't have roots, you don't have a community. Maybe I shouldn't bother. Everyone I knew and cared about is long gone. It feels too hard to start again."

"The important stuff is often difficult." I paused as I read through the ingredients list of a spell to triple energy. It wouldn't be enough, and I didn't have half the ingredients. "Is there anything useful in that book?"

Tansy shook her head. "I'm not sure any temporary spell will help you. We know how strong angels are. They need to be, since they go up against such devious creatures all the time."

I tapped a paw on the book as I studied Tansy. "What if I'm tackling this the wrong way round? If I give you more life force, how powerful could you become?"

Tansy blinked slowly at me several times. "I... well, I wasn't trapped in that old cemetery by mistake. I had the power to cause a lot of mischief, and I enjoyed making mischief, but it was never malevolent."

"Does that mean you're powerful enough to stop an angel?" I asked.

A worried look entered Tansy's eyes. "I'd have to take an awful lot of your life force, but I could slow one down. I don't want to hurt you, though. You've been so kind, and you've finally made life interesting again."

"I don't want to be hurt either," I said. "But I need to find Cherish's killer. We have three suspects, all of them angels, and I doubt the killer will come quietly. They've been hiding in plain sight all this time, and their truth is about to be revealed."

Tansy's gaze moved around the bookshelves. "I can do it if you're really sure."

"Just don't take all of my life force. So long as I have a little left, I can rebuild from that," I said.

Tansy shut the book she'd been looking through with a decisive snap. "Then let's go take down this angel together."

She reached out a paw, and I lifted mine to meet hers. Nothing happened for a second, but then a wave of both warm and chilly energy erupted between our paws. It flooded in all directions before swirling around Tansy, glowing pale blue. It gathered speed until it was almost a tornado.

She opened her mouth and drew the energy in. More and more spilled out of me, and as it did, I grew weaker, my eyelids growing heavy and my bones aching.

Just as I was about to tell Tansy to stop, she let go of my paw and staggered back.

I shook my head in disbelief. She looked magnificent. Her fur was sleek and glossy, her form radiant, and she seemed taller.

"Oh wow! That was the best ride I've ever had." Tansy spun in several circles, admiring herself. "Juno, your magic is extraordinary. There are so many flavors."

"I'm a patchwork of powers." I yawned, wanting nothing more than to curl up and sleep. I was also starving.

"Don't worry, you'll feel better soon." Tansy bounced on her paws. "I, however, feel extraordinary. Like I could take on the world and win."

"Let's just stick to bringing down one angel for now."

She giggled, and a flare of magic shot out of her. "Whoops! I'll have to get control of that. Your powers are deliciously spiky."

"They were once extraordinary," I said. "Can you handle it?"

"I'm not sure what exactly I'm handling, since there's such a mishmash in here, but I'll get used to it." Tansy twirled and giggled some more. "Let's go find ourselves a killer angel, shall we?"

I nodded, trailing after Tansy, who bounced around the library, laughing as more wild magic spiraled off her. She was the best weapon I had for bringing down an angel, and I had to hope it was enough.

We headed outside into the gloomy dampness, Tansy skipping ahead while I dragged my paws, struggling to focus and ignore the ache in every joint.

"Let's try the old cemetery," I said. "Aurek could have gone back there to speak to Cherish."

"They're not there." Tansy lifted her nose and inhaled sharply. "Don't you smell that? All the sweet cinnamon sugar in the air. The angels are close."

There was a loud boom, and the ground shook. A spark of golden light flared into the air, followed by another. Tansy took off like a rocket-propelled witch on a broomstick, and I failed to keep up as a soul-scrunching sense of exhaustion twisted through me.

Another boom almost knocked me off my paws

By the time I'd reached the corner, Tansy had stopped, her paws planted and her eyes wide.

In front of her, Lumiel and Aurek were fighting each other like their lives depended on it. Maybe they did.

Chapter 23

The air sizzled with power. Golden light flashed against the crumbling stone walls, each burst throwing jagged shadows across the street. I froze, my tail puffed, as Lumiel and Aurek circled each other like predators in a fight ring.

"You betrayed us!" Lumiel's shout cracked through the air like lightning. "You killed Cherish to hide your sins."

Aurek's wings flared, silver fire running along their edges. "I loved her. You're the one who twisted her work."

Lumiel raised her hand, and a spear of molten light shot from her palm. Aurek dove to avoid it, the beam slicing through a fence post and setting it ablaze. The acrid smell of burning wood filled the air.

Tansy darted in front of me, her fur blazing with pale blue energy. "Do you want me to take them down?"

"Not yet. I need to know why they're fighting." The ground vibrated as each strike of power sent cracks through the dirt. Feathers drifted like snowflakes, glowing faintly before fading into the smoke.

"Confess!" Lumiel yelled. "You hated that Cherish loved the halo fragments. She never loved you."

Aurek lifted his hands, his face strained. "You don't know what happened between us."

The clash of their magic sent a blinding pulse along the street. I threw myself behind a toppled crate, my fur standing on end. I rolled out and jumped up.

Tansy surged forward. "Stop! You'll tear the whole village apart if you don't rein in your magic."

Her magic exploded outward, a wild shimmer of icy blue cutting between the angels. Lumiel staggered, her wings flaring to steady herself. Aurek's glow dimmed, his chest heaving as if he'd run a marathon.

Behind them, I spotted Verity. She stood perfectly still. Her face was pale, her eyes fixed on the fight. Why wasn't she stepping in to help?

Lumiel regained her balance before glancing at me. "Aurek thinks he can fool us. Cherish warned me about him."

Aurek's expression faltered. "About me? Why? I did nothing wrong other than adore her."

"You murdered Cherish!"

"That's enough!" I shouted, my voice barely carrying over the roar of power that bubbled in the air, threatening to let out more whips of angel energy.

Neither angel looked at me as they readied themselves for the next round. They wanted to fight to the death.

A surge of gold light burst from Lumiel, striking Aurek in the chest. He cried out, spinning back as his wings folded in. He hit the ground, light spilling from the wound like falling stars.

Aurek groaned and rolled onto his side, clutching at the scorch mark across his chest. Smoke rose from the wound, curling in faint silver threads before fading into the damp air.

Lumiel advanced slowly. Her wings glowed like molten gold, lighting the street.

"Explain what's going on," I demanded.

"Aurek confessed to the murder," Lumiel said. "He admitted what he'd done and said he pushed Cherish when she refused him."

"That's not true." Aurek's voice was hoarse. "I would never hurt Cherish. I wanted to protect her."

"She didn't need you or your protection. More lies!" Lumiel raised her hand again, power gathering around her fingers. "You couldn't stand that she chose a demon's company over yours."

Aurek forced himself upright, his face pale. "You think love makes me a killer? You think I wanted her dead? Maybe it was you."

"Now you accuse me?" Lumiel shook her head. "Pathetic! You pointed the finger at Maelor, and when that failed, you tossed Yahir into the mix. Is panic making you slip up?"

"I'm not panicked. I'm... I'm heartbroken." Aurek remained on the ground, a hand pressed against his injury. "You wanted Cherish silenced because she didn't trust you."

"I know the truth!" Verity's voice cut through the tension as she stepped closer. "You confessed, Aurek. I heard you."

I blinked. None of this made sense. "Aurek really confessed to murdering Cherish?"

Verity nodded. "I overheard everything. Aurek admitted to meeting Cherish at the bell tower. He said he lost his temper when she denied him again, so he pushed her."

Aurek's eyes widened, panic flashing in them. "No! That's not what I said. I admitted I followed Cherish there, and we spoke before she went into the bell tower. I begged her to stop working with Maelor because it was so dangerous. But I never went up there with her. There really was a sick child who needed me. Lumiel twisted my words. She—"

Lumiel lunged, seizing Aurek by the front of his shirt. Golden light poured from her palms, sizzling against his skin. "You dare to call me a liar?"

I darted forward. "Bring that anger down to a simmer. You're burning him alive!"

Lumiel's head whipped toward me. Her eyes blazed with something that wasn't righteousness anymore. It was fury.

"He killed her!" she hissed. "Aurek said he couldn't stand seeing her with that wretched demon."

Tansy's energy flared behind me, a sudden gust of blue fire. "Back off, golden girl," she snarled. "You're not the only one who can throw light around."

Lumiel recoiled, then spread her wings wide, every feather glowing like a blade. "You think you can stop me, ghost?"

"I can slow you down." Tansy's grin was wild and bright. "I've got something special running through me thanks to Juno. Shall we test just how special it is?"

Lumiel's hands clenched as she glowered at Tansy. "You dare to use this dangerous misfit's power against an angel?"

Tansy's laugh had an edge of high-pitched hysteria. "What have I got to lose?"

"It doesn't have to be this way," I said. "Let Aurek go so I can question him. I understand your anger, but this is not the way to end things."

Lumiel shook her head as she raised a hand. "I'm done playing fair. No one played fair with Cherish. It's time the truth came out."

The air shuddered as blue and gold light collided in a furious arc. The blast knocked me back, my claws scraping the dirt as immense energy whined in my ears.

Aurek groaned from somewhere behind me, and I rolled over to see how he was doing. I wanted to reach him to make sure he could hold on, but the blasts of magic pulsing through the air would slice me in two.

Tansy's magic lashed out again and again. Shards of light spinning through the air, embedding in the dirt like glowing glass.

Lumiel's wings snapped open. She thrust both hands forward, golden power slamming into Tansy.

Tansy staggered, blue fire bursting from her fur. The smell of singed magic burned my booping snooter. She gritted her teeth, her paws sliding on the cracked stones.

For a heartbeat, angel and ghost cat light locked, neither giving way. The clouds tore open, rain falling in fat, hissing drops that evaporated as soon as they touched the glowing power.

Verity hadn't moved. She stood at the edge of the fight, watching in perfect stillness. Not even her wings twitched.

Tansy screamed, her magic breaking apart in wild streaks that shot off in every direction. Lumiel drove her back, step by step, the golden light swallowing the blue.

I hurried closer, crouched low, my heart pounding. "Tansy, stop! You'll burn yourself out."

"I can hold her," Tansy gritted out. Her eyes glowed brighter, almost white. "Just a little longer and I'll have her."

But the golden light surged again, pouring over Tansy like molten fire. Tansy shrieked. For one breath, I thought she'd vanished. Then she broke free and spiraled in the air, crashing into a wall with a crack of magic.

Darkness rushed in. The air sizzled. Lumiel's glow dimmed for a heartbeat, then she lifted her hand, ready to keep fighting.

Before she made the killing blow, the heavy beat of wings filled the silence.

Cythera dropped out of the sky. "What in the name of every blessed realm is going on here? I felt the angel energy from miles away."

No one answered. Tansy lay slumped against the wall, smoke curling from her fur. Lumiel stood rigid, her chest heaving, and her eyes blazing. Aurek was barely conscious, sprawled in the dirt. Verity looked away.

Cythera took in the scene, her wings flaring wide. She glared at me.

I jerked my head at the angels. "This fight had nothing to do with me."

She bared her teeth but snapped her attention to the angels. "Have you all lost your minds?"

"Aurek attacked first," Lumiel said. "I was defending myself."

"And I was defending Juno," Tansy croaked. "Juno, why are there two of you?"

"I had no choice," Lumiel said. "Aurek is dangerous."

"Enough!" Cythera said. Her voice dropped into that dangerous quiet that meant she was one spark away from losing her temper. "Everyone, return to the library. Now! I demand a full explanation."

With a groan, Tansy shuffled forward on her belly. Aurek tried to push himself up, but his legs gave out. Cythera grabbed him by the collar and hauled him to his feet like he weighed nothing.

"If any of you so much as light a fingertip with magic, I'll chain you to a sermon circle until the next century," Cythera growled. "I'm sick of having to clean up other people's messes."

"That's literally your job description," I muttered, as I ensured Tansy could stand.

"You put a sock in it." Cythera jabbed a finger at me as she held Aurek up. "Where ever you are, trouble swirls. Even when you're supposed to be stripped of magic and serving a sentence for almost blowing up an entire town, you meddle and make mishaps."

"My meddling has saved your feathery behind more times than you care to admit," I said.

"Stop talking, more walking." Cythera herded the angels in front of her, half-carrying Aurek.

I followed them, helping Tansy as she staggered. The rain hissed around us, washing away the scorch marks made by the blistering fight but not the tension.

My gaze flicked over the group of angels. One of them was broken. One of them had blood on their hands. But which one?

Something was very wrong here. But I was running out of ideas to figure out who'd murdered Cherish.

Chapter 24

"Let me hear the evidence." Cythera stood with her hands on her hips, glaring at all of us. "Just the facts. No embellishment." She was glaring at me when she made that last comment.

Lumiel stepped forward, her shoulders tight. "I obtained a confession from Aurek. He told me he pushed Cherish from the bell tower when she rejected his advances. He wanted her, but she knew she was too good for him."

"That's a lie!" Aurek moved toward Lumiel, but I jumped into his path.

"Do nothing foolish," I murmured. "Cythera isn't in the mood to be messed with."

"For once, Juno speaks sense," Cythera said. "Keep your tempers in check or I'll arrest you all."

"But Lumiel is accusing me of murder!" Aurek said. "I have to defend myself."

"And you'll get an opportunity to do so once I've heard from all of you," Cythera said. "Lumiel, what prompted this confession?"

Lumiel slid a glare at Aurek. "He said he had to clear his conscience, and coming back here stirred up too many bad memories."

"More lies," Aurek said.

"It's the truth," Lumiel spat out. "And I have a witness. Verity overheard Aurek confiding in me. I'm not sure what he expected me to do with the information, though. I could hardly keep it to myself."

"Is this true?" Cythera turned to Verity.

Verity nodded. "I remember Aurek always hanging around Cherish and trying to get her attention. She had a big heart, but it used to irritate her."

"Is there any truth that you had romantic feelings for Cherish?" Cythera asked Aurek.

"I... I cared deeply for her," Aurek admitted.

"And those feelings weren't returned?" Cythera asked.

"I knew they would be one day. I just needed to give her time," Aurek said. "We both know how important her career was to her."

Cythera's gaze flicked over him. "Your alibi for the night Cherish died?"

"I was helping a villager's sick child."

"Except your timings don't match up," I said. "There's a window of opportunity when you could have committed the murder."

"But I didn't! Why would I kill the love of my life?" Aurek said.

"The reason is irrelevant," Lumiel retorted. "You did it. You told me. We both heard it. I'm just glad we've figured out what happened to Cherish."

"Why were you fighting?" Cythera asked.

"Because I told Aurek what I intended to do," Lumiel said. "If he wasn't prepared to admit to being a cold-blooded killer, then I'd reveal all. That was when he attacked me, so I had to protect myself."

"Yet you almost killed him," I said.

"Isn't that what Aurek deserves?" Lumiel said. "He destroyed a magnificent angel. Cherish was one of a kind."

"Will you confess to me?" Cythera asked Aurek.

"I refuse to confess to something I didn't do," Aurek said, a desperate note in his voice. "These two are lying."

"We're helping get justice," Lumiel said. "Isn't that what this is all about?"

"This is getting us nowhere," Cythera said after glaring at everyone. "Let's take a time out to think this through."

I studied Cythera as she walked away, her hands clenched at her sides. She wouldn't appreciate me for doing it, but I followed her.

"Not now, Juno," she said, not looking over her shoulder. "I need to think."

"Something's wrong," I said. "You don't believe what you've just heard, do you?"

She pressed her finger to her lips and then gestured for me to follow her.

I hid my surprise as we headed deeper into the musty old library.

"What do you think about all of that?" she asked.

"Two angels against one," I said. "It's looking bad for Aurek."

Cythera nodded slowly. "I know Lumiel from somewhere. She looks so familiar, but I can't place her. I keep trying to remember how I know her face."

"Have you worked together?"

"It's not that. She's in a different division, adjacent to law enforcement, so there'd be no reason for us to have met professionally."

"She specializes in celestial relics," I said. "Perhaps you had her visit one of your many family homes to appraise your estate."

Cythera tutted. "Stop being an idiot."

"It's possible! I imagine a family of such high esteem has powerful, priceless relics in their possession. Perhaps I could borrow one sometime."

Cythera didn't smile. "Do you believe Aurek is guilty? He seemed so shocked."

"I'm unsure. He could be shocked because he knows the game is up," I said. "Maybe he wanted to unburden himself. I'd started asking questions, and it stirred up memories, along with a healthy dollop of guilt. Sometimes, guilt is too much to bear."

Cythera slumped into a seat, her gaze going to the window. "Cherish caused trouble for the family, but she was fun to be around."

"If that's true, I'm surprised you spent any time with her," I said.

"I wasn't always like this!" Cythera said. "But as I rose up the ranks, I had to become more serious."

"You can be fun *and* serious," I said. "There's room for both. Is that why you're having trouble with Maverick? He thinks you're being too serious?"

"He'd have us on a year-long vacation if I let him get away with it." Cythera sat back in the seat. "I don't want Cherish's killer to be an angel. It flips my worldview upside down, and that's messy enough."

I hopped onto the small table beside her and rested a paw on her arm. "Whoever did it, we'll have to charge them."

"*I'll* have to charge them. This has nothing to do with you," Cythera said.

"I imagine there's a lot of paperwork involved when charging an angel with murder."

"You can't even begin to imagine." Cythera groaned softly. "Why can't it have been the demon?"

"If it were Maelor, you'd have found out the first time you investigated," I said.

"I wasn't allowed near this investigation," Cythera said. "I wasn't high enough in the ranks to be considered for such a serious case. And with Cherish being family, I was too close to be impartial."

"And you're still too close." I hesitated. What I was about to say could get me in trouble. But what did I have to lose? "I'll make a deal with you. How about if I solve this, you let me come home?"

Cythera growled at me. "Don't make this all about you."

"You can see I'm doing good work," I said. "Even with barely any magic, I'm making a difference."

"You should have no magic," Cythera said. "And I know you're communicating with people back in Crimson Cove. It's the snow globe, isn't it? You're always breaking the rules."

"I'm gently bending them. And it's helping. I'm solving your cold cases," I said. "Maybe if you let me come back to Crimson Cove, I could carry on doing that."

"You've gotten lucky twice. That doesn't make you an expert in cold case crime," Cythera said.

"How about if I make it three times? Would that do it?" I asked.

Cythera closed her eyes for a second. "I make no promises, but I will talk to the higher angels."

I bounced up and down. "You won't regret taking me home. I'll be like your second shadow, making sure every case gets solved."

"Please don't make threats like that," Cythera said.

"How shall we proceed, partner?"

"We're not partners."

"We are for now."

"This is a mistake."

"This is purrfection," I said. "Like old times. So, what's the plan?"

Cythera huffed out a breath. "Let's make sure those three can't do anymore damage and then I'll patch up Aurek. After that, we need to rest. We'll pick this up tomorrow, and I'll decide what to do about our killer."

Rather than resting, I spent the night fixing the snow globe. Or trying to. I took it apart and put it back together. Added fresh fake snow, and tried a few spells I'd discovered on the shelves.

The connection was back, but it was horribly fuzzy, and Sage sounded like a robot. That didn't matter, so long as we could talk again.

I quickly updated Sage, who peered at me through the fuzz, her head tilted to one side.

"What's wrong with you?" she asked.

"I've been up all night, and it's almost dawn. I'm exhausted."

"It's not that. You look terrible. Dull. And I've never seen your eyes that color."

I waved a paw in the air. "It's nothing. I'll sleep when this case is resolved."

"And you think it has been resolved?" Sage still looked at me suspiciously.

"I'm hoping Aurek's been mulling things over during the night," I said. "We just need his confession."

"Maybe you don't," Sage said. "If Lumiel and Verity are trustworthy and they confirm he confessed, Aurek's in a heap of trouble."

"I need your help to check how trustworthy they are," I said. "We already know Verity concealed the issue with her family and her lack of job prospects, so her word isn't golden, but I know little about Lumiel."

"Lumiel is an unusual name for an angel," Sage said. "She won't be hard to track down. What do you want to know?"

"Her background. She doesn't work directly for Angel Force, but in an adjacent department, so she's not involved in solving crime or catching criminals," I said. "Cythera recognized her, but couldn't figure out where they'd met. Maybe she consulted with Lumiel on a case relating to angel relics."

"Relics are rare, so there'll be information on any joint working committees. There are always committees formed whenever any vaguely important matter is discussed," Sage said. "I'll have breakfast and then get Finn to look at the records."

"Could you do it before breakfast?" I asked. "I know it's a big request because I expect you've got an enormous plate of smoked salmon, scrambled eggs, and thick-cut slices of bacon waiting for you. But this is important. I want to make sure we're missing nothing."

"I'll have to wake Finn," Sage said. "And Vorana's still in bed, so there's no breakfast yet. I've already emptied the bowl of kibble, and I was planning on lying on her head, to make sure she didn't forget about me."

"As if you'd do such a terrible thing," I said.

"I can't help it. My stomach makes me do dreadful things."

"Good morning!" Tansy floated down and joined me on the desk. "I went out first thing and gathered supplies. I found a few dog chews that you might find edible."

I wrinkled my booping snooter. "Thanks. I'll have a sniff."

"You look remarkably well." Sage's eyes narrowed as she stared at Tansy. "Almost alive."

"Haven't you got a job to do?" I attempted to disconnect the snow globe, but Sage's face remained in full, fuzzy view.

"That's why you look so unwell!" Sage said. "Why did you give Tansy more life force?"

I knew Sage would be grumpy about this, which was why I'd kept it from her. "I wasn't strong enough to go up against the angels. Tansy stepped in."

"And I feel incredible!" Tansy said. "Juno's life force is extraordinary."

"It's her life force, not yours," Sage said. "Give it back."

"It's fine. I asked Tansy to take it," I said. "I knew she'd be more powerful than me."

"You can't keep giving away your life force!" Sage said. "You don't have an infinite amount."

"I don't need any more," Tansy said. "And I was happy to help. I fought the angels and almost won."

"Speak to Finn," I urged Sage. "That's the most urgent issue of the day."

"This conversation isn't over." Sage shot one more glare at Tansy and vanished.

"Is she always this grumpy in the mornings?" Tansy asked.

"Sage is protective of me," I said. "How about we investigate those dog chews?"

Tansy floated off the desk as I headed to the dated kitchen to explore the limited breakfast options.

"Do you think you'll get this case finished today?" she asked.

"I hope so."

"After you're done, we could explore Badger's Haze. I've been looking around myself, but it's no fun if I don't have someone to share things with."

"I know how that feels," I said. "I used to share everything with my wonderful witch, Zandra. I miss her dreadfully."

"That's terribly sad," Tansy said. "When do you think you'll see her again?"

"Soon. I made progress with Cythera last night. She's open to the idea of taking me back to Crimson Cove."

"Oh! You're leaving me?"

"It's nothing definite." I gathered my meager breakfast supplies and headed back into the library. "And you don't have to stay in Badger's Haze. Crimson Cove is nice. There are a few troublemakers in town, but there's a decent café, where you can get the best smoked salmon, and an amazing bookstore. A cute tearoom, too."

"I don't know." Tansy twirled in a circle before settling into a floating cat-loaf position. "I'll have to think about it. Are you sure I can't convince you to stay?"

"This is my prison, not a home," I said. "The sooner I get back to Zandra, the better."

Tansy sighed and closed her eyes.

By the time I'd munched my way through two meaty chew sticks, Sage's fuzzy face appeared.

"Did you speak to Finn?" I asked.

"He was helpful," Sage said. "He was just coming off night shift, so he accessed the records straight away. You need to read this."

Sage worked her magic and sent a sheet of paper through the globe. It crumpled up and came out sideways, but it arrived.

My mouth fell open as I reached the bottom. I now knew exactly who the killer was and why Cherish had been murdered.

Chapter 25

Cythera arrived at the library a second before I left to run to the inn, drag her out of bed, and give her the news. She must have read the information Sage sent through a dozen times before she finally looked at me.

"Where did you get this?" she asked.

"The source isn't important," I said, "but it's the truth, isn't it?"

"How did I forget something so important?" Cythera asked.

"You have a lot on your mind," I said. "A failing marriage, an Angel Force division to run. And I can tell you're not sleeping."

"Stay out of my personal business." Cythera gripped the paper. "Follow me. Let's gather everyone together and get this over with."

I dashed after Cythera as she yelled for the others, noticing Tansy peeping over the top of a book stack, staying out of the way. It was a sensible move.

Lumiel and Verity had slept in an empty room on the upper floor, while Aurek stayed on my floor, recovering on the mouse-nibbled couch. They all shuffled into view. Aurek looked worse for wear, but his chest wound was better.

"I have proof of who the killer is," Cythera said with a sigh.

Lumiel, Aurek, and Verity had settled around the same table, although Aurek was at the far end, keeping his distance from the others.

"I can't believe you need any more proof," Lumiel said with a snap of sharpness.

"You be quiet," Cythera said. "Okay, this is what's going to happen—"

"If I may interrupt," I said. "It makes sense to go over all the suspects. It wasn't just these angels in the frame for murder."

"I want this done so I can go home," Cythera said.

"Then allow me to be brief, and you can do all the necessary arresting," I replied.

Cythera's hands flexed repeatedly, and her wings quivered. She jerked her chin up and gestured for me to talk.

"You must know it was Aurek, right?" Lumiel's expression grew concerned. "You have two reliable witnesses who heard him confess. What else do you need?"

I hopped onto the desk and paced along it. "When I reopened this cold case, there were six suspects or witnesses questioned by Angel Force following Cherish's murder. I'd like to go over them. We'll start with Nix Busby, since she's the only one with a solid alibi."

"She was the hostess, wasn't she?" Lumiel asked.

I nodded. "Nix was charming, and used to be a social spinner. She kept a piece of jewelry for far longer than she should, causing tension with Cherish."

"Who would kill for a piece of jewelry?" Verity muttered.

"Some people have," I said. "But Nix is innocent. She was at a spa on the night of the murder."

"Which means it was Aurek," Lumiel said.

I ignored her. "We then have Yahir Hallow. He interested me after Aurek said he saw Yahir going into the bell tower on the night of the murder."

Aurek nodded. "He was there, but I'm uncertain he went inside. He just vanished. Until Lumiel turned feral—"

"Trust nothing Aurek says," Lumiel said. "He changes his lies daily. Just arrest him and be done with this. Ignore what he tells you about Yahir."

"Yahir was interested in the halo fragments," I said. "And he would have made a convenient patsy. He was a loner, and he admitted to being near the bell tower that night."

"You think it was him?" Verity glanced at Lumiel. "I suppose it could be Yahir."

"No. Evidence in Yahir's old house showed how much he enjoyed headstone rubbing," I said. "The only reason he was there was to enjoy wandering among the headstones and make fresh rubbings, not to murder Cherish."

"Which means what?" Verity asked. "You're planning to arrest Aurek?"

"It means it was one of you," I said. "Although... a suspect is missing. Where is Maelor?"

"You now think it was Maelor?" Verity asked. "I'm so confused."

"Maelor was the prime suspect for a long time," I said. "So, I'm sure he'd like to know our thoughts on his involvement. But a reliable informant has confirmed an angel whisked Maelor out of the library while he was healing."

"That doesn't matter," Lumiel said. "Aurek did it!"

"I'm sure it matters to Maelor," I said. "Who will tell me where he's been hidden? I hope no harm has come to him."

"What does it matter if one pesky demon goes missing?" Lumiel sighed. "Cythera, can't you take control? I don't know what this cat is doing. Isn't she here because she's a criminal?"

Cythera lifted the piece of paper Sage had sent through, but I darted in before she could speak.

"We need to know where Maelor is," I insisted. "Is he in any danger?"

"Of course he's not!" Lumiel said.

"And you know that how?" I asked.

Lumiel's cheeks flushed. "Fine. I moved him. I didn't like the thought of him wandering around once he'd recovered, especially since I believed he was the killer."

"Until Aurek conveniently confessed to you," I said.

"There was nothing convenient about it," Lumiel said. "I was there during a moment of weakness and got lucky."

"Where have you put Maelor?" Cythera asked.

"In the bell tower," Lumiel said with some reluctance. "I thought it was fitting he was trapped there, left alone with his thoughts about the trouble he'd caused Cherish."

"Then we go there," I said. "It's only fair Maelor hears this. He'll be worried that we're on the verge of arresting him."

"He's a demon. He should be arrested," Lumiel said.

"Check your prejudice," I said. "It's tarnishing your halo."

"You were wrong to move Maelor," Cythera said.

Lumiel shrugged. "He's only a demon."

I hissed, but Cythera hushed me with a hand wave.

"We need to check on Maelor," I said. "He may not be important in your eyes, but he was injured and could be in pain."

"I agree. I'll take us to the bell tower," Cythera said. "Can I trust the three of you to join us, or do I need to drag you there?"

"Of course you don't!" Verity said. "We want this solved as much as you do."

I looked up expectantly at Cythera. "Does that mean I have the privilege of flying with you?"

"I should make you run, but I want this solved fast so I can leave. Don't dig your claws into my feathers, or I'll forget to hold on to you."

I wriggled my butt. This would be an experience.

Cythera scooped me up, settled me against her chest, and we left the library. We waited for the others to join us, then Cythera crouched and took off like a hungry toad after a juicy fly, shooting into the sky.

The wind was so sharp it made tears pool in my eyes. Cythera smelled of warm sugar, with a hint of honey swirled through it, and I resisted the urge to snuffle into her warm feathers. That would make things weird.

We landed a few moments later on the bell tower ledge. Cythera dropped me inside, barely giving me time to ensure I landed on my paws, before climbing in after me.

Aurek, Lumiel, and Verity joined us a second later in a whoosh of heavenly-scented white feathers.

I looked around the gloomy gray stone bell tower. There was a space where the bell must have hung, but it was empty.

"Where's Maelor?" I asked.

"He's in that chest over there," Lumiel said. "He's tied up so he can't harm us."

I hurried over and cracked open the chest. Maelor's anxious face peeked out at me.

"Don't worry, you're not in trouble," I said. "I just found out you were here. How are you feeling?"

"Sore and hungry," Maelor said. "What's going on?"

Cythera strode over and helped him out, slicing through the glowing bindings with a hand swipe. Maelor stretched, rubbing his wrists where he'd been shackled.

He peered fearfully at the angels. "What are you all doing here?"

"First off, freeing you," I said, "and then letting you know you're no longer under suspicion of murdering Cherish."

His mouth dropped open, then he snapped it shut. "You found out who killed her?"

"Yes. And we thought you'd like to know," I said.

"Of course! Let me at them. I'll make them sorry," Maelor said.

"You stay where you are, foul demon," Lumiel said. "You're lucky you're still alive."

"He is, isn't he?" I said. "You're fond of attempting to kill anyone who stands against you."

"That's unfair!" Lumiel said. "I only use my power for good."

"You tried to murder Maelor in the inn."

"That was an act of necessary force to protect another angel," Lumiel said. "I don't regret doing that. And I'd do it again."

"You also tried to murder Aurek after claiming he'd confessed to killing Cherish," I said.

"Again, I was protecting myself." Lumiel pulled back her shoulders. "Verity will support me."

Verity looked worried, but she nodded.

Maelor stood up straighter. "Are you suggesting one of these angels killed Cherish?"

"Yes. And although Lumiel and Verity want us to believe it was Aurek because of his unrequited love for Cherish, that's untrue," I said.

"You're delusional!" Lumiel said. "And I've been looking into your background. You're a criminal, banished here for your gross misdeeds. We can't take anything you say seriously."

"An angel," Maelor breathed out. "That makes sense. That night, there was a blast of pale light."

"When Cherish was fighting with someone in here?" I asked. "You saw that from the ground?"

Maelor ducked his head. "Um... something like that."

"Explain," I said. "What did you see? The light wasn't in your statement."

Maelor shuffled his feet through the dust. "I... I told the angels I saw Cherish fall, and that I ran to save her."

"Is that not what happened?" I asked.

"I don't want to get in any trouble," Maelor said.

"Typical demon," Lumiel muttered. "Always lying."

"Go on," I said to Maelor. "What happened that night? What did you see?"

Maelor's small gray tongue flickered across his lower lip. "I wasn't outside. I was in the tower when the fight happened. Although it wasn't much of a fight."

"You saw Cherish's attacker?" I asked.

"No! They stayed in the shadows, and their voice was distorted. They must have done it to hide their identity."

"What did they say?" I asked.

"They were angry because of me," Maelor said.

"What did you do to make them angry?" Cythera asked.

"If I tell you the truth, please don't send me to prison," Maelor said. "I had to do it, you see. I didn't know if Angel Force would protect me. You do your best, but it's not enough, especially not against the demons I had links with."

"You double-crossed Angel Force, didn't you?" I asked. "Cherish's killer was angry because they found out you'd reported back to the demons while working with her."

Maelor nodded. "The demons I stole the halo fragments from found me. They sent someone with a message to say if I didn't get inside information on Angel Force, that would be the end for me."

"What did you do?" I asked.

"I told Cherish. She said she'd protect me, and I had nothing to worry about. But, well, we all know what Angel Force is like. They're slow to respond, and demons act quickly. I was protecting myself."

"You sniveling liar," Lumiel snapped. "You're going back to prison."

Maelor cringed and ducked his head.

"Hold on a moment," I said. "You were in the bell tower when Cherish's attacker arrived. Then what happened?"

"They attacked! This blast of brilliant energy flooded out toward me."

"Toward you?" I asked. "Not Cherish?"

Maelor nodded. "I thought I was a goner, so I turned away. But then Cherish was falling, and then... she was gone. And so was her killer."

I looked at Lumiel and Verity. Neither of them met my gaze.

"Verity, you spoke so proudly of Cherish and said you wanted to be just like her," I said. "That was why you joined Angel Force, wasn't it?"

"Sure. That's true," she mumbled.

"But you lied about being up for promotion. In fact, a review of your record revealed you've never been promoted. And there's a reason for that, isn't there?"

Verity looked away and didn't speak.

"Cherish's actions embarrassed your family," I said. "Her choices tarnished your record, too. Do the angels whisper about you being from the same family as Cherish? Her eccentricities meant you suffered."

"That's a motive for murder," Cythera said, her expression stern.

I nodded. "With Cherish dead, you hoped to end the gossip and slurs."

"It wasn't me!" Verity said. "The night Cherish died, I wasn't near the bell tower. I have an alibi."

"You don't have the best alibi," I said. "It would have been simple to sneak out of your room, come to the bell tower, attack Cherish, and then return before anyone noticed you were gone."

Verity glanced at Lumiel. She glared back at her, a silent message passing between them.

"I wasn't sure we'd ever figure this out until we took a closer look at you, Lumiel," I said.

"This is ridiculous. You're passing judgment over everyone," Lumiel said. "I suppose it had to be my turn eventually."

"I always leave the best till last," I said. "Or should that be the most devious? And thanks to Angel Force keeping excellent records, we know about your past. How long have you pretended you still work for Angel Force?"

She jerked back as if hit by something. "I do work for Angel Force! I'm in the Celestial Relics Division."

"You used to be." I looked up at Cythera. It was time she filled in the missing pieces.

"I knew I'd met you before, but I couldn't place your face," Cythera said. "We've never worked together, and I just couldn't figure it out."

"You're mistaking me for someone else," Lumiel stuttered.

"I sit on plenty of committees and have passed judgment on many angels," Cythera said. "Sometimes the faces blur, but Juno got an associate to check our records."

"Hold on," Verity said, the color gone from her face. "Lumiel no longer works in the Celestial Relics Division?"

"Don't listen to them," Lumiel said quickly. "They're making this up."

"Why would they lie about that?" Verity asked.

"The twisted magic in Badger's Haze has gotten to them," Lumiel said. "It's filled their heads with lies. Or they're in league with this foul demon."

"This village does dull an individual's senses," I said. "But Cythera knows you because she fired you for improper conduct."

Verity thumped her hands on her hips. "Is this true? You know I can find out if I contact someone in your division."

"It's a misunderstanding," Lumiel said. "I'm figuring it out. I'll be back at work by the end of the month."

Verity sucked in a sharp breath. "If you no longer work in the Celestial Relics Division, how will you get me that new job you promised me?"

"Oh! You promised Verity a change of role? Something with more money and prospects, perhaps? In exchange for what?" I asked.

"Supporting your lie that Aurek confessed to murdering Cherish?"

"Don't say anything else," Lumiel said, her furious words directed at Verity.

"Is that what happened?" Aurek asked. "I wondered why Verity was sticking up for Lumiel and telling the same lie."

Verity's anxious gaze flicked around the group. "How do I know you're not lying about Lumiel?"

Cythera handed her the sheet of information Sage had sent through. "Here is the decision of the committee I sat on. It recommended Lumiel be expelled from the Celestial Relics Division. She was caught attempting to sell a rare object."

"That was never proven!" Lumiel glowered at Cythera.

Verity read through the information several times before turning slowly to Lumiel and shoving the paper in her face. "Not only are you a killer, but you're also a rotten, stinking liar!"

Chapter 26

Lumiel's gaze flicked from Verity to Maelor and then to Aurek. She was looking for an avenue to blame someone else, but she was out of options.

"Verity did it," Lumiel finally said.

"It was you! You lied to me. You had no plans to help me." Verity chewed on her bottom lip for a few seconds. "I'm sick of being the office joke. No one takes me seriously. I just push paper around a desk and then go home and stare at a blank wall, wondering what I'm doing with my life. Lumiel offered me a way out. She promised me that if I stood by her, I'd be guaranteed a move into her department where she'd help me get up the ladder."

"I believe you," I said. "Lumiel, what really happened that night?"

Lumiel's gaze went to a window, but Cythera blocked it. "Don't even think about it. It's time you told the truth."

A shudder ran through Lumiel, and she sagged against the wall. "It was all his fault."

"Who?" I asked.

Lumiel looked at Maelor. "I kept telling Cherish not to trust him, but she wouldn't listen."

"So, you acted," I said. "You came to the bell tower to stop their partnership."

"I had to confront them together, to question Maelor and show Cherish how deceitful he was."

"It was you!" Maelor said with a croaky snarl. "You were the one hiding in the shadows."

"You be quiet. I have nothing to say to you," Lumiel said.

Maelor stepped forward. "You didn't come to the bell tower to kill Cherish, did you? You were after me. You hated me the second you set eyes on me. Why?"

"You should have accepted your fate and taken the hit," Lumiel said. "But Cherish was too noble for her own good, and she got in the way. That blast was meant for you! I had to get rid of you. You're rotten to the core. You corrupt everything you touch, and that includes Cherish. She wasn't thinking straight, and that was your fault!"

"You're saying Cherish's death was an accident?" I asked.

"Yes! I never meant to hurt Cherish. I admired her work." Lumiel breathed heavily, hatred glowing in her eyes as she glared at Maelor.

"But you also coveted the halo fragments," I said. "Were you angry because she wouldn't hand them over straight away?"

"That's irrelevant. We'd have found a way to work together," Lumiel said. "If I'd hit this devious demon and killed him that night in the bell tower, you'd have all given me a medal."

Cythera sighed and shook her head. "I've heard enough. Lumiel, you're under arrest for Cherish's murder."

***

I'd had a full night of rest, leaving Cythera to tidy the loose ends and process Lumiel. Two angels had collected her, and she was in holding before going to spend an incredibly long time serving an overdue sentence.

Once she knew the game was up, she'd admitted everything. Cherish's murder. Planting the halo fragment in Yahir's home to confuse the investigation. Attacking Maelor when he was asleep at the inn.

Aurek had gone home, while Verity had more questions to answer, and was likely to lose her job and possibly get a stretch inside for providing false information to shield Lumiel.

Maelor should have taken time to heal, but he'd snuck off as soon as he could, mumbling about never wanting to meet another angel again. Poor demon. I'd felt sorry for him.

"What's the plan?" Sage asked from the snow globe, her form still fuzzy, despite my best efforts to make repairs.

"That's for Cythera to decide," I said. "I'm hoping the fact I've solved a relative's murder makes her see me more favorably."

"And if it doesn't?" Sage asked.

"There are more cold cases to solve. But I need to be back in Crimson Cove," I said. "It's where I belong. How's everything back home?"

"So-so," Sage said. "But there's no point in troubling you with the details until you can do anything about it."

Tansy, who'd been lounging on the desk, lifted her head. She jumped down and slunk away.

"Where are you off to?" I asked.

Tansy didn't look back. "Your grumpy angel friend is coming. And she doesn't like me."

"She's barely seen you to form an opinion."

"Even so, I don't want to cross swords with her. Angels bring me out in hives." She floated to the top of a bookshelf and vanished from sight.

A few seconds later, Cythera marched into the library. She must have had a busy night because she looked unusually exhausted and had wrinkles in her uniform.

"I'm leaving," she said by way of a greeting.

"I trust you're taking me with you," I said. "My bags are packed."

"I've told you I'll put in a word with the higher angels, but that's the best I can do," Cythera said.

I sighed. How unsurprising not to get a straight yes or no answer from an angel. "How did everything go with Lumiel's transfer?"

"She's being dealt with. But I've had to step back." Cythera scowled at a stack of books as if it had said something offensive to her. "It's a case for those above my pay grade. They'll keep me informed, though."

"I should think so. Cherish was your family."

There was a crash in a nearby book stack, and Tansy rolled into view. She scrambled up and tried to dash away. Her panicked gaze landed on Cythera, and they locked eyes.

Cythera took a step back, her gaze widening. "It is you! I thought I was seeing things. A trick of my imagination. How... how are you here?"

"No, it's not me. You're thinking of someone else." Tansy turned away, her form flickering. "I'll be going. Don't want to get in the way of important business. And this sounds super important."

Cythera continued to stare at Tansy, her mouth open.

"Do you two know each other?" I asked.

"We definitely don't know each other." Tansy's ears were flat against her head.

"This makes no sense. You're still here after all this time," Cythera spluttered out.

"I really don't know what you're talking about," Tansy said.

Cythera's head jerked back, and she glanced at me before smoothing her hands down the front of her shirt. "Oh yes, of course. Maybe I made a mistake. You look familiar, that's all."

A glimmer of magic sparked across Tansy, and her eyes narrowed. "I suppose I would look somewhat like a familiar to you, wouldn't I?"

"What's going on?" About a million unspoken words flickered between these two, and I had to know why.

"It's nothing. I need to leave." Cythera turned but didn't walk away. Instead, her head seemed to twist against her will, and she stared at Tansy again.

"Tansy, what's happening?" I asked. "You clearly know Cythera."

Tansy shrugged. "These angels all look the same to me."

"Why was she surprised that you're here after such a long time?" I persisted. "What does that mean?"

Cythera turned around slowly, and the glare she gave Tansy was sharp enough to fell a goblin at twenty paces.

"Cythera, did you trap Tansy in the old cemetery?" I asked. "You passed her sentence for some crime she committed. Is that how you know each other?"

"It's not relevant," Cythera said. "Are you coming with me to Crimson Cove? I won't offer again."

My head whipped up, and my heart gave a pitter-patter of startled joy. "You said you'd put in a good word with the higher angels. I can't just leave."

"You can. Let's go. We'll sort things out once we're home." She gestured for me to join her.

I took a step toward Cythera. "Why the sudden change of heart?"

"You should go," Tansy said. "You've got your freedom. Congratulations. It's what you always wanted, isn't it?"

"It is. More than anything," I said, "but I also want to know the secret you share with Cythera. The secret that's so big, she's willing to flout higher angel rules and spring me out of Badger's Haze."

"It happened a long time ago. It doesn't matter now. We've learned our lesson, and that's all you need to know. Are you coming or not?" Cythera asked, looking everywhere but at Tansy.

I sat and wrapped my tail around my paws. "Tansy, every time Cythera showed up, you vanished. You didn't want her to see you. If it's not because she imprisoned you in the cemetery, why do you keep hiding?"

Tansy drew in a slow breath that seemed to go on forever.

"Don't say a word!" Cythera's tone was glacial. "You'll only do more harm."

"To you, maybe." Tansy's expression hardened. "It's time the truth came out."

"What truth?" I whispered.

Magic flickered across Tansy again, and she drifted toward me, although her attention was on Cythera. "Angels are supposed to be benevolent creatures. Kindness, full of light, and welcoming to all. However, we know that's not true."

"No magical being is ever perfect," I said.

"The angels tell everyone they are, but they carry envy in their hearts. Do you know what they're most envious of?" Tansy hissed softly at Cythera.

"That not everyone has to wash their clothes every day because they don't dress head to toe in white?" I asked.

A small, hard smile crossed Tansy's face. "Familiars. Angels want familiars."

"That's definitely not true," I said. "Cythera despises me sitting on her desk, shedding fur, and borrowing food from the Angel Force kitchen."

"It is true," Tansy said. "We know how powerful the bond is between a magic user and their familiar. I've seen you visibly decline because you're not with your bonded witch."

I tilted my head. "Angels want familiars to make them stronger?"

"It makes perfect sense. So many angels go into law enforcement," Tansy said. "Imagine what it would be like if they had a familiar watching their back, just like you do with Zandra. It would be a game changer."

I glanced up at Cythera, whose hands were clenched and her shoulders tense.

"Is there anything you'd like to add to this?" I asked.

Cythera shook her head.

"The records of what happened are sealed and redacted," Tansy said. "But if you dig hard enough and bribe the right people, you'll learn all about their dirty little secret."

"But you're prepared to tell me?" I persisted.

"I'm done hiding," Tansy said. "And I'm done being punished for something that wasn't my fault."

Cythera jabbed a finger at her. "What you did to Badger's Haze was your fault. You didn't have to do that."

"I was making a point!" Tansy snapped back, magic crackling across her fur.

"You hurt people. Ruined lives. Destroyed the prospects of an entire village!" Cythera's wings fluttered. "That is unforgivable."

"Tansy! You put a hex on this village?" I asked. "You're behind all the troubles?"

"The angels underestimated me," Tansy said with a sniff. "After they tossed me aside as one of their many failures, they trapped me here. I was punished because of what they did! I taught them a lesson, so they'd regret abandoning their experiment."

"Experiment?" I asked.

"I wanted to show them what they'd missed out on," Tansy said. "Do you know what they did? They turned their backs not only on me but on this entire village. It was disgusting. It showed their weakness and that their hearts are full of pride, not goodness."

I took a few seconds to process this information. Tansy believed the angels wanted familiars, but there was no natural way to form a bond between an angel and another magical being. What magic had they used to attempt such an impossibility?

"Did you force spells on Tansy so she'd bond with you?" I asked Cythera.

Cythera looked away and shook her head.

Tansy stamped her paw on the floor. "Answer Juno. Or are you too afraid to speak the truth because it will show how corrupt you are? Your heart isn't pure. It's black and festering with shame. And so it should be."

"I... I wasn't leading that project," Cythera mumbled.

"You were a face on the committee who made the decisions," Tansy said. "You were a chosen angel who decided what would happen to your failures."

"There was a committee to make familiars for angels?" I asked. "What a surprise."

"We're always transparent in our work," Cythera said.

I snorted a laugh at the same time as Tansy.

"So, a group of angels got together to figure out how to force bonds on magical creatures so they could have sidekicks to help with their work," I said. "Is that right?"

Tansy nodded. Cythera appeared to be frozen in place.

"But you failed," I said. "You had to have failed."

"The project was quickly closed." Tansy's voice dropped. "All the forced bonds corrupted. And we died. I died!"

A breath whooshed out of me. "The angels hid all their failures here?"

"Just me. I was the last attempt to make things work," Tansy said. "I died because the bond corrupted, but the angels were so desperate to make it work that they resurrected me. When they discovered that no amount of twisting and manipulating energies would get me to bond with anyone, they imprisoned me here."

I turned wide eyes to Cythera. How had she allowed this to happen?

Tansy went on, "So, to prove I wasn't useless and I still had abilities, I hexed Badger's Haze."

"Cythera, say something in your defense," I said. "You knew about this?"

Cythera's gaze went to the window, and she sighed. "It's not a proud moment in Angel Force history. We haven't tried again."

"I should say it's not," I said. "What were you thinking?"

"Exactly what Tansy said. Law enforcement is a tricky business, and we needed extra support. There was a war raging against multiple covens of dark crones, and the angels were called in to support them. But we were losing! We weren't getting good-quality recruits through the academy fast enough, and everything was falling apart. Having familiars seemed like the perfect compromise."

"You can't force a bond if it's not meant to be," I said, my heart a stuttering mound of pounding shock. "Angels have enough power without having a familiar."

"But they wanted more," Tansy said. "Greedy, gluttonous, gloriously awful angels."

A thought struck me so hard, I staggered back. "Cherish figured this out, didn't she? She knew something odd was going on in Badger's Haze."

"That was the big secret she'd uncovered." Tansy nodded. "Cherish was an incredible angel, and she was mortified when she learned the truth about the brutal nature of those who are supposed to protect us."

"Because you gossiped to her about what we did!" Cythera said.

"I was telling my truth to the only angel I still trusted." Tansy stamped her paw again. "You shattered that trust! You and the rest of those mindless committee idiots who thought you had the right to mess with us."

"I was planning to visit Cherish and figure things out," Cythera mumbled. "Make her understand why we did it. But then she died."

"And that was when all the angels turned away from Badger's Haze and abandoned everyone," I said. "Not just your broken experiments, but all the residents. Cythera, shame on you."

"It wasn't just me!" Cythera threw up her hands.

"Let me guess. You were following orders, the same as you always do," I said. "Which is the reason Tansy was imprisoned for so long, and I was wrongly sent here for doing a good thing."

Cythera opened her mouth to protest, but then snapped it shut. Her hunched figure told me everything I needed to know.

"I am sorry for what I did to Badger's Haze," Tansy said. "I didn't mean for things to go so far, but once the corruption started, I couldn't contain it. Being trapped in the cemetery gave me limited means to get out and fix things."

"Can you fix things now?" I asked.

She nodded. "It'll take time, but I'm sure I can."

"Will you?" I asked.

Tansy looked at Cythera. "That depends on my status. Will I get my freedom back?"

I turned to Cythera and stomped toward her, thumping a paw on her boot. "You know what Angel Force did to those familiars was brutally wrong and cruel."

Cythera closed her eyes for a second. "It was never meant to happen that way. It's something we deeply regret, but we didn't realize it would go so terribly wrong. And there was a war! We needed an edge."

"Potentially incredible familiars died because you lusted for extra power," I said.

Cythera licked her lips but nodded. "It was wrong."

"Maybe we should revisit Cherish's case," I said. "You have as good a motive as anyone now for wanting her dead."

"Don't be ridiculous!" Cythera snapped.

I glared at her until she looked away. "You're just fortunate that Lumiel confessed."

"I'd never kill a family member," Cythera said.

"She would if the committee she was on told her to," Tansy sniped.

Cythera drew back her shoulders. "Are you coming with me or not? I have a meeting in an hour."

"I'm absolutely coming with you," I said. "On one condition."

"Which is?"

"We take Tansy. She's free to leave Badger's Haze."

"No! She's a troublemaker," Cythera said. "You've been living in Badger's Haze, so you know how corrupt she is. Tansy destroyed this village."

"Tansy admits what she did was wrong, but she was lashing out, desperately hurt and miserable because she was forced into an experiment against her will. An experiment you condoned."

"I'll behave," Tansy said. "And I will work out a fix for Badger's Haze. I would like to be free, although I'm not sure where I'll go."

"Come to Crimson Cove," I said.

"Not Crimson Cove!" Cythera protested.

I ignored her. "You'll find all sorts of wonderful magical misfits there. I have an amazing group of friends, and you'd be welcome to join us."

"That sounds incredible," Tansy said. "I'll need to come back here, though, and right my misdeeds. Badger's Haze was once an incredible place. It can be again. I'll get Midnight and the others to help."

"I'll work with you too," I said. "And Angel Force will be happy to give generous support to this endeavor, won't they, Cythera?"

Cythera mumbled something under her breath, but she was nodding.

"Maybe start a committee," I said. "We expect financial, emotional, and magical support. Nothing is too much for Tansy's project. Hey, that's what we'll call it. The Tansy Project. And we need a law enforcement presence back here. A good-sized team. Tansy will supervise them until everyone is bedded in."

"Oooh! I get a team? That's exciting." Tansy bounced up and down on her paws. "And I love the name. I'll need to recruit, too. And get a magic boost. There's so much to think about. But to do any of that, I need my freedom."

"Is Tansy free?" I asked Cythera. "We can all go home to Crimson Cove?"

Cythera's lips pressed together before a defeated sigh slid out of her nose. "So long as we work out how to return Badger's Haze to a prosperous village and remove all traces of the hex, Tansy can leave."

Tansy squeaked. "I'm free! I'm finally free after so many miserable decades trapped here. And you can go home too, Juno!" She danced around, her magic pinging off my booping snooter and making it itch.

I joined in the dance as I looked around the library and let out a contented sigh. Life was looking up again. I always knew this day would come, so long as I held on to a thread of hope.

"Stop dancing!" Cythera said, a flicker of her old grumpiness returning.

"Join us!" I said. "Today we celebrate."

"You might not be celebrating for long." Cythera grabbed my tail and pulled.

I whirled around and hissed. "Keep your hands off my tail!"

"You're not listening to me." Cythera made a grab for my tail again.

I tempered my joy when I saw how serious Cythera was. "What's wrong?"

"Before we leave, there are things you need to know about what life is like back in Crimson Cove..."

Are you ready for the next adventure?
Well... you have options!
If you're new to the world of the Magical Misfits
Mysteries and this trilogy is your first encounter
with Juno and her magical sass, you can:
Dive into the world with **Every Witch Way but
Juno**, where our feisty feline finally goes home. But
things aren't the same as she left them.
Or...
Enter Juno's world from the very beginning with
Every Witch Way but Ghouls (this is book one in
the Magical Misfits Mysteries.)
Every Witch Way but Ghouls (available in ebook,
paperback, and audiobook.)

About the author

K.E. O'Connor (Karen) is a mystery author living in the beautiful British countryside. She loves all things mystery, animals, and cake.

When she's not writing, she volunteers at a local animal sanctuary, reads a ton of books, binge watches mystery series, and dreams of living somewhere warmer.

To stay in touch with the mysteries, where the killer always gets caught, justice is served magic style, and the familiars talk, head to her website, join her weekly newsletter, and grab free ebooks.

Newsletter: www.keoconnor.com/freebooks
Facebook: www.facebook.com/keoconnorauthor

www.ingramcontent.com/pod-product-compliance
Lightning Source LLC
Chambersburg PA
CBHW050607190726
48283CB00007B/2319